SKINFLICK

A RINEHART SUSPENSE NOVEL

A RINEHART SUSPENSE NOVEL

A Dave Brandstetter Mystery

SKINFLICK

Joseph Hansen

HOLT, RINEHART AND WINSTON
New York

Published by Holt, Rinehart and Winston, 383 Madison Avenue,
New York, New York 10017.
Published simultaneously in Canada by Holt, Rinehart and
Winston of Canada, Limited.

Library of Congress Cataloging in Publication Data
Hansen, Joseph, 1923–
Skinflick.
(A Rinehart suspense novel)
I. Title.
PZ4.H247Sk [PS3558.A513] 813'.5'4 79-11077
ISBN 0-03-048931-8

First Edition

Designer: Lucy Castelluccio
Printed in the United States of America
10 9 8 7 6 5 4 3 2 1

In memory of Doctor Dreadful
who left too soon

SKINFLICK

A RINEHART SUSPENSE NOVEL

He parked in sunglare on a steep narrow street whose cracked
white cement was seamed with tar. The tar glistened and looked
runny. He sat a minute longer in the icy draft from the dashboard
vents. They'd been blowing since he got into the car twenty
minutes ago, but the back of his shirt was soaked with sweat. And
it was only ten in the morning. Los Angeles didn't get like this
often. He hated it when it did. And this time it was holding on. It
had been brutal at the cemetery three weeks ago. His father's nine
widows had looked ready to drop. The savage light had leached the
color from the flowers. The savage heat had got at the mound of
earth from the grave even under its staring green blanket of fake
grass. He'd stayed to watch the workmen fill the grave. The earth
was dry. Even the sharp walls of the grave were dry. What the hell
was he doing remembering that? He switched off the engine,
grabbed his jacket, got out of the car.

The door fell shut behind him. In the oven air, he flapped into
the jacket. He crossed the street. The house stared at him blind and
sunstruck over oleanders. The curtains were drawn. The garage

doors were down. The lots were hard to build on here. House front and garage front were only a step back from the street. On the short uptilt of driveway in front of the garage doors the tape the police had put down to mark where a dead body had lain had been pulled up. But adhesive from the tape had stayed on the cement, and summer dust and street grit had stuck to it and renewed the outline in grime. Tire tracks crossed it but there were no other stains. Gerald Ross Dawson hadn't bled. He'd died of a broken neck.

Cypresses crowded the front door, cobwebby, untrimmed. He groped behind them till his fingers found a bellpush. He pressed it and inside quiet chimes went off. Dave knew the four notes. Sometime in his early teens, without quite understanding why, he had dogged the steps of a handsome boy addicted to Pentecostal meetings. The Dawson doorbell chimes picked out the start of a gospel chorus, "Love Lifted Me." No one came to the door. He let the second hand go around the face of his watch once and pushed the button again. Again the notes played. Again no one came. He tilted his head. Did he smell smoke?

A path went along the front of the house, cement flagstones, the moss on them gone yellow and brittle in the heat. Arm raised to fend off overgrown oleanders, he followed the path. At the house corner, it turned into cement steps with ivy creeping across them. He climbed the steps, sure now that he did smell smoke. At the top of the steps, in a patio where azaleas grew in tubs and where redwood furniture held dead leaves, a dark, stocky boy of around eighteen was burning magazines in a brick barbecue. He wore Levi's and that was all. The iron grill was off the pit and leaned at the boy's bare feet. He acted impatient, jabbing with an iron poker at the glossy pages blackening and curling in flames the daylight made almost invisible.

He was half turned away from Dave. He was a furry kid, fur on his arms, even on his feet. A magazine was in his hand. He kept starting to toss it into the pit, then drawing it back. He wiped sweat

2

off his face with his arm and Dave saw the title of the magazine
—*Frisco Nymphets.* The color photo was of three little girls, aged
maybe ten, without any clothes on. The boy poked savagely at the
flames, making a small sound that reached Dave like whimpering.
The boy flapped the magazine in a kind of frantic indecision, then
dropped it into the flames. Dave could feel their heat from here.
He didn't want to go closer but he did.

"Good morning," he said.

The boy whirled, mouth open, eyes wide. The poker fell out of
his hand and clattered on the charred brick edge of the pit. Without
taking his scared gaze from Dave, he groped out behind him to try
to cover the magazines with his hands. That wasn't going to work.
He backed up and sat on the magazines. One slid away, off the
barbecue surround, onto the patio flags. *Six-to-Niners.* The naked
female children on this one held yellow ducklings. The boy
snatched it up and threw it into the fire. The flames choked out and
sour smoke billowed around them. Dave coughed, waved hands in
front of his face, and backed off, jarring a thigh against a redwood
table.

"Come over here," he said.

"What is it?" the boy gasped. "Who are you?"

"My name is Brandstetter." Dave handed the kid a card. "I'm
an insurance investigator. It's about Gerald Ross Dawson,
deceased. I came to see Mrs. Dawson."

"She's not here." The boy coughed and wiped his eyes with his
fingers. He frowned at the card in the smoke. His brows were thick
and black and grew straight across without a break. "She went to
the funeral home. Some women came from the church. They went
to see my dad."

"You're Gerald Dawson, Junior, then—right?"

"Bucky," he said. "Nobody calls me Gerald Dawson Junior."

"Were you cold?" Dave asked. "Did you run out of briquettes?"

"I don't understand you," Bucky said.

"That's funny fuel. Where did you get those?"

3

"I found them in—" But Bucky changed his mind about that answer. "They're mine. I'm ashamed of them. I wanted to get rid of them. Now was the first chance I had."

"Magazines like that cost a lot of money," Dave said. "How many were there—ten, a dozen? That's fifty, sixty dollars, maybe more. You were lucky to get that kind of allowance. Your father must have thought a lot of you."

"And look how I repaid him," Bucky said.

"You can only use so many Bibles," Dave said. "But shops that sell these don't cater to kids. It must have been hard to get them. Doesn't that count?"

"Not now." Bucky shook his head. "I hate them." Tears were in his eyes and not from the smoke this time. The smoke was trying to drift off. "He was so good. I'm such a sinner."

"Don't make too much of it," Dave said. "Everybody has to be eighteen sometime. When's your mother coming back?"

"Don't tell her I was doing this," Bucky said.

"I only ask questions," Dave said.

"The police already asked them all," Bucky said. "Why do you want to start it over again? It's too late. Everything's too late. They even kept his body downtown ten days." He turned sharply away, trying to hide that he was crying. He went back to the barbecue and poked blindly at the smoldering paper. Smoke huffed up again. He blew at it, making a wet sound because of the crying. Small flames licked up. "They're finally going to let us give him his funeral tomorrow. Can't you just leave us alone?"

"Where was he the night he was killed?" Dave asked.

"I don't deserve to be called by his name," Bucky said. "He never did anything dirty in his life. Look at these. I'm always dirty. I pray and pray"—he jabbed at the flaming magazines, outraged, despairing—"but I can't be clean. Look at me." He turned suddenly, flinging out his arms. Flakes of pale ash had caught in the black wool of his chest and belly. "Covered with hair. Anybody can see what I am. An animal."

4

"Genes," Dave said. "Did he often stay out all night?"

"What?" The boy blinked. His arms lowered slowly. It was as if Dave had wakened him from sleepwalking. "No. Never. Why would he? Sometimes he was late. But that was church work."

"Do you know what kind?" Dave said.

"This neighborhood"—Bucky began shredding up a magazine and wadding the shreds and throwing them hard into the flames —"isn't a fit place for Christians to live. It isn't a fit place to bring up children. Stuff goes on in that park there isn't even any name for. Have you seen those smut shops, those pervert bars, the movies they show? Filthy." He ripped at the magazine. "Filthy places, filthy people. Burn!" he yelled to the fire. "Burn, burn!"

"He was trying to clean it up?" Dave said.

Bucky went guarded and sulky. "I don't know. You know where he was. The police found stuff on his clothes. He'd been where there were horses. He'd made an enemy of Lon Tooker."

"Keyhole Bookshop," Dave said.

"Right. And he's got horses where he lives, in Topanga Canyon. That's why they arrested him. Don't you know anything?"

"I read the police report," Dave said. "That's why I'm here. It doesn't satisfy me."

"You? What difference does that make?"

"Fifty thousand dollars' difference," Dave said.

Under the soot that smeared his face, he turned a pasty color. "You mean you could hold back his life insurance? That's to put me through college. That's to keep my mom. She can't work. She's handicapped."

"I don't want to hold it back," Dave said, "but a couple of things are wrong and I have to find out why."

"The only thing that's wrong is he's dead," Bucky said. The tears came back. "How could God do that? He was God's servant. He was doing God's will."

"Lon Tooker was in his shop till midnight."

The fur boy scoffed. "The creep who works for him says. Any-

5

body who'd work in a place like that—what would they care about lying?"

"The shop hours are posted on the door," Dave said. "Noon till midnight weekdays. And if he kept those hours, then he couldn't have been home to his horses till two or after. Topanga's a long drive from here."

"What's that mean?" Bucky began shredding another magazine. "My mom didn't find my dad's body till she went out to get the *Times* in the morning."

"But the medical examiner says he died between ten P.M. and midnight."

"I got home at midnight," Bucky said, "from basketball practice at the church. He wasn't there. I would have seen him." Another wad of glossy paper went into the fire. For a second, a naked fifth-grader looked seductively over a skinny shoulder at Dave, then blackened and vanished. "Lieutenant Barker says the medical examiner could be wrong."

" 'Could be' doesn't mean 'is,' " Dave said.

"He got home, got out of the car to unlock the garage, and Lon Tooker jumped him," Bucky said. "The stuff from the horses rubbed off Tooker onto him."

"Nifty," Dave said. "Did you hear the struggle? Where do you sleep?"

Bucky jerked his head at corner windows. "There. I didn't hear anything. I was tired. I slept hard." He ripped at another set of pages. "Anyway, what kind of struggle do you think there was? Tooker got him from behind and snapped his neck. You learn how to do that in the Marines. Tooker was a Marine in World War II."

"It looks easy in the movies," Dave said.

"It happened," Bucky said.

"Tooker would have to be fifty-five," Dave said. "Your father was ten years younger."

"He didn't know anything about fighting," Bucky said. He poked at the burnt paper and big loose fragments sailed up through

6

the heat like sick bats. They settled up above on the ivy-covered slope. "He was a Christian."

"Not a soldier of the Lord?" Dave said.

"Are you laughing at him?" Bucky turned with the poker in his hand. "What are you? An atheist or a Jew or something? Is that why you don't want my mom and me to have his insurance money? Because we're born again?"

"If he was trying to open the garage door," Dave said, "where were his keys? They weren't in his pocket. They weren't on the ground."

"Tooker must have taken them," Bucky said.

"He was searched," Dave said. "So was his shop. His home. His car. They didn't find those keys."

Bucky shrugged and turned back to jab at the fire. "Tooker threw them away someplace. What good would they be to him?"

"Exactly," Dave said. "So why take them at all?"

"Why don't you get off my case?" Bucky said. "Don't you think we've got enough trouble, my mom and me, without you coming around and—" Down on the street, a car door slammed. The poker clanked again. Bucky turned pasty again. He stared alarm at Dave. "There's my mom, now. Oh, look, listen—don't tell her about the magazines. Please."

"Maybe you should quit for now," Dave said. "Put them away. Wait for another chance."

"If you don't say anything"—Bucky retrieved the poker—"it'll be okay. She won't come up here. It's too hard."

"Then I'll go down there," Dave said.

The smoke hung caustic in the slanting street. No wind stirred to take it away. It kept crawling down the hillside. It lodged in the shrubbery. A tall, wide-hipped woman came out of the garage where a tan Aspen showed an I FOUND IT bumper sticker. The woman dragged her right foot; a cane hung over her arm. She wore a new tan double-knit pantsuit over a new cocoa-color synthetic shirt. She'd had her hair done. It was iron gray. Effortfully she stretched up for the garage door and dragged it down, clumsily shifting aside just in time for it to miss her. She turned toward Dave and stopped. An eyelid drooped. So did a corner of her mouth. But she got her words out sharply.

"Who are you? What do you want?"

He went to her, spoke his name, handed her his card. "When a policyholder dies by misadventure, we investigate."

"Where's my son?" She looked up. "What's that smoke?"

"He's burning trash," Dave said. "I've talked to him."

"He's only a child," she said. "You had no right."

"I'm not a police officer," Dave said.

"What did you talk to him about? What did he say?"

"That he thinks Lon Tooker killed his father," Dave said. Across the street, window-fastenings snapped. French doors opened beyond shaggy treetops. "Maybe it would be better if we talked inside."

"There's nothing to talk about," she said. "The police have arrested the man. I guess that means the district attorney must have been satisfied he was the right one. Why is it unusual that Bucky should think so?"

"It's not unusual," Dave said. She had to be close to sixty. It wasn't just that a stroke had left her half paralyzed. Flesh sagged loose beneath her jaw. Her skin was a web of wrinkles. There were liver spots on her hands. Gerald Dawson had married a woman almost old enough to be his mother. Bucky had been a last-chance baby. He said, "But it's too easy."

She gave her head a shake that made the loose lip quiver. "There's nothing easy about it. Everything about it is hard. Death is hard. Loss is hard. Even for Christians, Mr."—she glanced at the card—"Brandstetter. God sends these things to test us. But knowing that doesn't make the tests any easier to bear." She narrowed the eye whose lid she could control. "What are you doing here? You haven't brought a check from the insurance company. Have you brought another test?"

"Where was he that night, Mrs. Dawson?"

"On the Lord's business," she said. "I don't know the particulars."

"Who would know? Someone at the church?"

She started toward the door, using the cane, dragging the foot. "They've already said not. Maybe Reverend Shumate." Keys rattled in her free hand. She clutched at a cypress to haul herself up the short doorstep. She poked the key at the door. "It seems very hard that he should have been killed, going about his Father's business."

Dave said, "At the bank, his statements show he wrote a couple of large checks lately. Do you know why? Are his canceled checks here?"

"At his office," she said. "The girl there paid all the bills. It was simpler." The door swung inward. There was a breath of lemon-scented furniture polish.

Dave asked: "Why did he have birth-control pills in his pocket?"

She stopped moving, hand on the door latch. Slowly, painfully, she turned. She twisted her mouth in a wince of disbelief. "What? What did you say?"

"Among the items the police found in your husband's pockets —wallet, credit cards, the usual—was an envelope from a pharmacy on the Sunset Strip. And in the envelope was a folder of birth-control pills. The prescription was written to Mrs. Gerald Dawson. Would that be right?"

"The Sunset Strip." It was only six or eight miles west, across town. But she said it blankly, the way she might name someplace in Afghanistan. Then she didn't say anything more. She simply kept her gaze on Dave's face. She seemed stunned.

He said, "The doctor's name is Encey. Is he your doctor?"

Her face twitched. "What? Encey?" Then suddenly answers chattered out of her. "Dr. Encey." She nodded. "Yes, yes, of course he's my doctor. That's right. The pills," she said. "Yes, of course. Gerald promised to pick them up for me. I'd forgotten. In all the terrible things that happened, I'd forgotten about the pills."

"I can understand that," Dave said.

"I have a headache," she said. "It's this dreadful heat. Excuse me."

And the living half of her dragged the dead half inside and shut the door.

He dropped out of the expensive Hillcrest neighborhood down twisting streets past old apartment courts where doors were enameled bright colors and sported new brass knockers, where windbells hung in the trees, and where lissome young men in swim trunks clipped hedges or soaped down little sports cars at the curbs. Then, another level lower, he passed rickety wood-frame houses in need of paint, where radios blared mariachi music through rusty window screens, and little brown Mexican kids swarmed in yards where no grass grew.

He braked the Electra at Sunset for a red light. Across the broad curving stream of traffic lay the park with the little lake, the ducks in the rushes, the muggers in the bushes, the sunburned tourists rowing battered little skiffs and peering through Instamatics at the glass skyscrapers beyond the tops of palms. When the light turned green, he swung left, making for Bethel Evangelical Church. But he changed his mind because the door of Lon Tooker's shop hung open under a red-and-white tin sign, KEYHOLE BOOKS. It took a while to find a tilted street he could swing into and back up out of, but at least there was no parking problem. Except for a corner Mexican grocery, the rest of the flat-roof one-story brown-brick store buildings along this stretch held businesses that flourished only after dark.

The carpet inside Tooker's place was thick enough to make it dangerous for anybody with weak ankles. It was gold color. Flocked gold-color wallpaper rose above the bookshelves. Gold-color paint was new on a ceiling from which hung fake crystal chandeliers. Plastic-wrapped magazines lay back at forty-five-degree angles on low shelves. The color printing was sharp but the subjects were monotonous. Spread legs, lace underwear, girls lifting massive breasts while they leered and coaxed. Or youths displaying bulky penises. No little girls. But then, this wasn't all the stock. A few feet farther on, stairs carried the thick, gold carpet upward between frail wrought-iron railings. Thumps seemed to be coming from there. Dave went up.

Fake fur covered deep square chairs. On wood-grain Formica coffee tables glistened green bubble-glass ashtrays. Here the shelves were packed—except for those already stripped by the youngster with knobby elbows who was dumping magazines, big picture books, and paperbacks into cartons. He was sweating so hard his shoulder-length blond hair looked as if he'd just brought it out of a swimming pool. He didn't wear a shirt. Pimples the size of boils flamed across his coat-hanger shoulders. He winced at Dave for a second before turning away again for more books.

"Ah, Christ, did she leave that door open? Look, dad, we're closed."

"Forever?" Dave asked.

"You got it." The boy dumped a stack of magazines into a carton and worked at the carton flaps, tucking one under another, to keep it shut. "No more Keyhole Books."

"Not even a going-out-of-business sale?"

"Mort Weiskopf over on Western's taking the stock."

12

"What's the hurry?" Dave dropped into one of the fur chairs. "Money for lawyers?"

The skinny boy hitched at his pants. "What do you know about it? Where do you come from?"

"The company that insured Gerald Dawson's life."

"Yeah, the money's for lawyers. That son of a bitch goes right on making trouble even when he's dead. You know he came in here with a bunch of potbelly bastards from that church one night and tossed the place? Threw books all over. Dumped paint on the rugs."

"That was the time to get the lawyer," Dave said.

"We couldn't prove who it was. They wore masks. I mean, we knew but the lawyer said they had alibis—they got this club at the church, right? They were all there. On their fat knees. Praying. For us sinners."

"It could have been six other people," Dave said.

"Except Dawson was yapping orders," the kid said. "Quoting the Bible. Sodom and What's-its-name? All that shit. It had to be Dawson. Nobody else had a voice like that. High and gravelly, and cracking all the time."

"But the lawyer said you couldn't get him?"

"Dash, across the street, tried it." The kid grunted, squatting, heaping up magazines. "The guy who owns the Oh Boy! Lives halfway up the hill. Sees a funny light outside in the middle of the night. Comes out. His VW is on fire. Sitting there in his driveway. On fire all over. He knew it was Dawson and his vigilantes. But no, they were having a meeting, singing hymns. Shit." He heaved tottering to his feet under a load of coated paper and dropped the load into another carton. "And the cops don't care, you know? Fag-bar owner's car burns up. That's funny. To them that's funny, right?"

A young woman in a man's white shirt that she'd tied under her breasts, and in very small white shorts, stopped at the head of the stairs. She was honey color.

13

"We're closed for business," she said. She tried to lift the carton the kid had closed, squatting for it, trying to rise up. "Jesus. What's inside—bricks? We're not taking the building, are we?"

The skinny kid didn't look at her. "You want the cartons half full, say so."

"I don't want them at all," she said. "This is Lonny's idea. He gets so panicky."

"They lock you up for murder," the kid said, "it's probably hard to stay calm. Are you going to load the car or not? You want me to carry, you fill the cartons?"

She picked up the carton without seeming effort. Her thighs were boyish and hard-muscled. "If he didn't buy horses, he wouldn't need money." She turned with the carton and saw Dave again. "You look like you could afford a couple of overpriced palominos. How about half a dozen? Come on, beautiful. It's for a good cause."

"The seat's too high off the ground," Dave said. He got up. "Here. I'll carry that." She started to protest and he told her, "It's for a good cause, right?" Her car was two doors off in a weedy vacant lot between brick walls spray-painted with street-gang graffiti. The car was one of those eighteen-thousand-dollar Mercedes sports models with the roof that dips. The trunk space was limited. She was going to have to make a lot of trips to Western. "The kid says Dawson is the vigilante chief."

"We all say so," she said, "but we can't prove it. The straights went after the vigilantes when they ripped down the bushes in the park. Pensioners. Housewives with kiddies. They ruined their park to keep the fags out of the shrubbery at two in the morning. At two in the morning, who cares what's in the shrubbery? And they couldn't nail them. So what can us pre-verts and smut peddlers expect?" She slammed down the trunk lid.

"Did your friend Lonny take the short route?"

She stared. Her eyes were flecked with gold. "What does that mean?"

"Get fed up waiting for justice?" Dave said. "Eliminate Dawson before Dawson eliminated him? Replacing that kind of carpeting could run into money if you had to do it very often."

"You know what kind of a man Lonny Tooker is? The kind of a man that sets broken bird's wings."

"Hitler loved dogs and babies," Dave said.

"He's a big, strong guy. He could kill anything alive with his bare hands. A bull, an elephant."

Dave put a hand over her mouth. "You didn't say that."

Her eyes widened. "Oh God. No. I didn't say it. What I meant was—he's gentle. A big, soft gentle dreamer. A lover. He loves everything that moves and breathes. He's dumb as hell but he wouldn't hurt anybody, let alone kill." She looked at her watch. "Come on. I have to hurry."

Dave trotted after her. It was too hot for that but he did it anyway, shedding his jacket as he ran. At the top of the stairs, he asked the skinny kid, "Was Dawson in here the night he was killed?"

"Nobody was in. It was a dead night. About five stragglers. But nobody was here after ten. Just Lon and me. We played gin."

"Who won?" Dave laid his coat on the stair rail.

"I can answer that." The girl had another carton and was half-way down the steps with it. "Lon won. He wins any game you win by getting low points."

"She's right," the skinny kid said. He patted stacks of paper-backs inside a carton. He stood, and treated himself to a look at a magazine, flapping the sleek, flesh-tone pages over, but not, Dave thought, really seeing the tangles of bodies in the photographs. The kid slapped the magazine shut and tossed it into a carton at his feet. He reached for the cigarette Dave had lighted. Dave passed it to him. The kid blew the smoke out appreciatively. He took another deep inhalation and handed the cigarette back. "You know," he said, "those creeps are hypocrites, you know?" He tipped his head, frowning. "Is that the right word? Anyway—what I mean—they

15

cream themselves over this crap. They pretend it shocks them, but you can see from the way they lick their lips, they're practically coming in their pants."

"What kind of masks?" Dave asked.

"Ski masks. I kid you not. They were drooling. They want to look at this stuff like anybody. Only they didn't have the nerve to walk in and ask for it and pay for it and like that. Oh, no. They toss the place, wreck it, make out all they want is Lon to get out of the neighborhood, see?"

"I don't know," Dave said. "Do I?"

"Sure you do. We put the stock back on the shelves. And guess what? Some magazines are missing." The kid snorted a cynical little laugh and reached for Dave's cigarette again. "Somebody couldn't control theirself."

"Pictures of little girls," Dave said.

The kid squinted. "Yeah. How did you know?"

"Just a wild guess," Dave said.

"Not all real little," the kid said. "Up to about twelve or something. Creepy, though—right? I mean, acting like they're Mister Clean?" He looked at the cigarette. "You want the rest of this?" Dave shook his head. The kid sucked in smoke and let it out with a question. "What do they do—pass them around at those prayer meetings of theirs?"

"Did Lonny kill Dawson?" Dave asked.

"Over ten bucks' worth of magazines wholesale?" The kid bent and stubbed out the cigarette in an ashtray. "Forget it."

"Over trying to wreck his business," Dave said.

"You don't know Lon. All he wants is to play his guitar and ride his horses."

"Does he come to work in the clothes he rides in?"

"No way. Never. Always right out of the shower, always neat and, what do you say, crisp? You smell horse in here? Never. Look, he's stupid, but sweet stupid, okay? Not mean stupid. You should hear the songs he writes. They make 'Feelings' sound like a Nazi

16

march or something. And what he never wants is trouble. Not with anybody."

"He picked a troublesome business," Dave said.

"To help people feel good nobody cares about."

"A kindly philosopher," Dave said.

"Yeah, well, the money's not that bad. And Lon hates to worry about money. It gives him headaches."

The girl called from below, "Car's loaded. I'm off."

"Don't drive under any trucks," the kid called.

"Did Lon go home that night?" Dave asked.

"If you had something like her waiting for you"—the kid jerked his lank-haired head at the stairs—"where else would you go?"

"She wasn't there," Dave said. "According to the police report, Karen Shiflett didn't reach Tooker's Topanga Canyon place until morning. She'd been with a sick brother at a hospital all night."

"He's a hype. He tried to OD. Yeah."

"So there's no proof Lon didn't kill Dawson."

"He set himself up," the kid said glumly. "Asshole. He should never have called the cops after that raid and told them it was Dawson."

"He couldn't foresee Dawson would be murdered."

"He could stop believing in uniforms," the kid said.

3

Bethel Evangelical Church was a clumsy hulk on a backstreet corner. From outside, the stained-glass windows looked muddy. The structure was old frame, and the dazzling new white paint that covered the shiplap siding didn't hide that the lines were all off kilter. What didn't lean sagged, and what didn't sag bulged. Pigeons waddled in and out of latticework high on a bulky steeple. They made pigeon noises. Dave came down the off-line cement steps he'd climbed to a pair of brightly varnished doors that wouldn't open. He winced up at the pigeons. Then he walked a strip of new cement along a sun-hot side of the building to another set of steps that went up to a door.

It was marked OFFICE and he opened it and stepped into cool air that smelled of mice and mildew. The place had stood empty and neglected for too long, but now new paint was in here too, a sprayed fiber soundproof ceiling. The same sort of deep carpet covered this floor as the floor at Lon Tooker's sex shop, only here it was holy blue. Wood-grain Formica made the desk in front of him glossy. It held a white pushbutton phone. Beside the desk was a sleek electric typewriter. Slick-paper color pamphlets on alcoholism, abortion, divorce, narcotics, stood in a plastic rack.

Behind the desk, a closed door had a brown plastic tag on it incised in white, PASTOR'S STUDY. He knocked on the door. Silence. A third door faced the one he'd come in. He opened it and was on the platform of the church auditorium. There was a square pulpit. Back of a railing were blue-plush theater seats for the choir. Organ pipes went up, the new gilt on them looking crusty. On the carpeting, plastic buckets waited, filled with cut flowers. For the funeral tomorrow of Gerald Dawson? He turned around. Out in the stained-glass dimness, varnished pews ranked a half acre of newly carpeted flooring. The emptiness was big.

His father's widows would have liked it. The tiny, crowded mortuary chapel hadn't let them sit far enough apart in their gloves and veils. None of them had dared fail to show; attorneys, executors, were there as witnesses. Absence would have conveyed indifference to the millions in cash and shares Carl Brandstetter hadn't been able to take with him. To have claimed not to know of his death wouldn't have convinced anyone. A long obit had appeared with his Viking-handsome picture in a weekday *Times* business section, recounting his single-handed building of one of the nation's life-insurance giants, Medallion. A Sunday *Times* article had focused on his splashy not-so-private life. His death from a heart attack while driving his Bentley on a two A.M. freeway was on every TV newscast.

Dave pictured the widows scattered in the jammed pews. One had stood through the ceremony, at the rear, beside a fake twelfth-century baptismal font. Evelyn, if he remembered rightly. The stepmothers of his childhood were clear enough in his mind, whether he wanted them there or not. The later ones blurred. Most had been buxom blonds in their twenties who'd run to fat on their alimony payments, waiting for this funeral, when Dave had seen them together for the first and only time. But three or four, like the latest and last, Amanda, were dark. One of these, nineteen, his own age at the time, he'd almost fallen in love with. Lisa.

When she'd taken his hand in her small gloved one between flowering shrubs outside the mortuary doors, and turned up to him big doe eyes that didn't glow anymore, it was as if he saw her on old movie film, faded, scratchy. Her voice hardly reached him, and then it sounded ugly, guttural, all the long-ago romance of the foreign accent now scrap. Lines marred the beautiful bones and shadows of her face. She'd been slim and soft. She'd become scraggy. They'd tried reminiscing—this ballet with Eglevsky, that Heifetz concert at Hollywood Bowl—but not for long. His father's ashes weren't the only ones in that damp, fern-murky little chapel. Ah, the hell with it.

"Hello!" he shouted. To no one.

Outside, at the rear of the church, where the sun hammered an almost empty blacktop parking lot, he found a set of steps down into an areaway. The door at their foot opened into a hallway of small meeting rooms with steel folding chairs, now and then a piano, little red chairs, a hamster rustling in a box with a wired front. A sound reached him from double doors at the end of the hall. Loud slaps. They were swing doors. He pushed through them and was in a gymnasium where a tall man of maybe forty, jacket off but still wearing his tie, was dribbling a basketball, pivoting, shooting. Dark sweat patches were under his arms and down his spine. He saw Dave and let the ball ricochet off the backboard and bounce to the other end of the court where long church-supper tables with folded-up legs leaned against the wall. The man came at a lanky jog to shake Dave's hand. He panted. He mopped his face with a handkerchief.

"Tuesday morning ordinarily nobody comes," he said, "nobody phones. I sneak down here to see whether it's come back or not. I had it in high school. I got a college scholarship on it—Wheaton, Illinois. But by the time the term started in the fall, I'd lost it."

"You probably grew," Dave said. "It happens."

The tall man compressed his mouth and shook his head. "I don't know. Eye-hand coordination, whatever—it was gone, simply gone. I was frantic. I worked. I prayed. It never came back." He laughed at himself. "In my secret dreams, one of these days I'll come down here and it will be back the way it was." He raised a warning finger and his grin was a kid's. " 'Call no man a fool,' " he said.

"All right." Dave watched him pick up a seersucker jacket that matched his trousers. "My name's Brandstetter. I'm investigating the death of Gerald Dawson. For Sequoia Life and Indemnity." He almost said Medallion, a twenty-five-year habit. But the morning after his father's death, he'd cleared out his handsome office high up in Medallion's glass-and-steel tower on Wilshire. This was his first free-lance assignment. "The police don't seem sure of where he was the night he was murdered. That bothers me."

"I don't know, myself," the tall man said.

"You're the minister here?" Dave said.

"Lyle Shumate," the tall man said. Jacket over his arm, he headed for the double doors. "We're going to miss Jerry Dawson. A born leader. True Christian."

"He had a men's group." Dave followed the preacher. "They didn't meet that night?"

"Their meetings were frequent but not regular." Shumate went into the kindergarten room under pink and blue crepe-paper streamers and crouched to squint at the hamster. It came out of a heap of wood shavings and looked at him, bright-eyed. It was chewing. Shumate touched a bottle hung on the wire of the cage. There was water in it. "You're okay, my friend," he said, and stood.

"The Born-Again Men," Dave said.

"They'd get together by telephone," Shumate said, "and set a time." He pulled open the outside door. Heat and glare struck in. He let Dave go out before him and pulled the door shut. "But they didn't meet that night." His soles went gritty up the steps. "Some of our kids have a gospel rock group. They used the Born-Again Men's room that night." He climbed to the door marked OFFICE and again motioned Dave through it ahead of him. "It must have been noisy in the basement that night."

"Basketball practice too," Dave said.

"You know about that?" Shumate said.

"But you weren't here," Dave said. "You can't tell me whether Bucky Dawson practiced with the team."

"If he says so, he did." Shumate went into PASTOR'S STUDY, sat behind a desk that didn't look busy, and waved Dave to a chair upholstered in nubby blue-and-orange tweed to match the curtains and carpet.

"It's a team that works hard," Dave said. "According to Bucky, they didn't quit till almost midnight."

"We lost the playoffs last year to the Nazarenes from Arcadia," Shumate said. "We don't want that to happen again. If Bucky told you they worked till midnight, they worked till midnight. He's the straightest boy I know. Intelligent, well-balanced, decent. We all look up to Bucky—youngsters and grownups alike."

"He acted troubled when I saw him," Dave said. "A lot of torment about sex."

"What?" Shumate stared, mouth working at a smile of disbelief. "We can't be talking about the same boy. I've heard Bucky on the subject—no one could be better informed and clearer headed. He talks to youth groups all the time. Sex, narcotics, abortion, alcoholism. All those matters the church used to stick its head in the sand about when you and I were kids. It's a different world. Those things have to be faced squarely and honestly today and dealt with."

"And Bucky Dawson faces them squarely and honestly and deals with them?" Dave said.

"And helps other youngsters to do so." Shumate nodded. Then

he frowned and sat forward. "You're not trying to say that Bucky was somehow mixed up in his father's murder."

"Not if he was here playing basketball," Dave said. "The medical examiner says his father was killed between ten and midnight. And I've got a problem with that. Bucky didn't find the body when he got home. His mother found it in the morning. Now, look, Reverend—"

"Call me Lyle," Shumate said.

"The police checked with the other men in Dawson's group, and they each told the same story. They didn't meet that night. They didn't go out on one of their vigilante forays—"

"Vigilante forays?" Shumate's face went stiff.

"You've heard about them. Harassing the customers going in and out of the massage parlors, the gay bars? Ripping out the shrubbery in the park? Setting fire to Dash Plummer's automobile? Throwing books around at Lon Tooker's place, pouring paint on the carpets?"

"There's no proof of any of that," Shumate said.

"No legal proof, no," Dave said. "But you're not a lawyer or a judge. You're a minister."

"The law has fallen into Godless hands in our country," Shumate said. "It protects evildoers. Decent people haven't a chance. I'm talking about human law. But there's a higher law—God's law."

"And Dawson and his raiders carried out that law—right? And they didn't see anything wrong with lying to the police about their activities, covering up for each other, because the police are trapped in a corrupt system, isn't that it?"

"I don't know about that," Shumate said stubbornly. "I never heard it from Jerry or any of his group or from anyone else in this church. Only from outsiders, barging in here with wild charges, people totally depraved, every one of them."

Dave gave him a one-cornered smile. "I didn't think See-No-

23

Evil, Hear-No-Evil, Speak-No-Evil were Christians," he said. "I thought they were monkeys."

"You and I both know where the evil is in this neighborhood," Shumate said, "and it's not in Bethel Church."

"Did Dawson have a high-pitched, gravelly voice?"

Shumate blinked. "You could describe it like that."

"Easy to mistake for anyone else's voice?" Dave asked.

"You couldn't miss it," Shumate admitted. "Why?"

"He captained the raid on Lon Tooker's shop," Dave said. "Six men. Masked. They all claimed afterward they were downstairs here, praying. Now—if they lied to the police that time, they could have lied to them about Dawson's whereabouts on the night he was killed. Now, I'm asking you—did they have some action planned for that night?"

"And I'm telling you," Shumate said, "I don't know. If Tooker believed Jerry Dawson raided his shop, then why doesn't that suggest to you what it suggests to the police—that Tooker killed him?"

"For one thing, the raid took place ten days before Dawson's death. Why would Tooker wait?"

"Maybe Jerry went there that night?"

"A witness says no. And Dawson didn't see relatives that night. He didn't see friends. He didn't come here to the church. He wasn't at his business. Where was he? Whom did he see and for what reason?"

"His life was an open book," Shumate said. "I knew the man almost as well as I know myself. He was uncomplicated, straightforward. He had a successful business, gave God the credit, contributed generously to this church—and not just in money; in works, good works of all kinds."

"He was around here a lot," Dave said. "All right, then tell me this—did you notice anything out of the ordinary about him before he was killed? Was there any change in him? Did he make any out-of-the-way remarks? Was he—?"

"Hold it." Shumate frowned, pressing his temples with his fingertips, eyes shut. "There was something. Yup. I'd forgotten about it." He gave Dave a look that was half smile, half frown. "You must get high marks in your job, Mr. Brandstetter."

"I've been at it a long time," Dave said. "You're about to break the Dawson case wide open, are you?"

Shumate laughed. "I don't think so. But it did seem a little odd at the time, a little out of character. It was after Sunday-morning service. In the parking lot. I went around there, wheeling an elderly parishioner in his chair. He only gets out on Sunday. It cheers him up to have a man to talk to for a few minutes. He's surrounded at home by a wife and three daughters. And after he was in the car and I was putting the wheelchair into the trunk, I noticed Jerry Dawson in a far corner of the lot talking to a big young fellow in a cowboy hat, cowboy boots."

"A stranger," Dave said.

"I'd never seen him before. He had been inside for the service, though, way up in the balcony at the back. He was noticeable because he has a beard." Shumate smiled faintly. "Like an Old Testament prophet. And bright blue eyes. Black beard, black brows, blue eyes."

"You didn't hear what they were talking about?"

"No, but I think they were quarreling. The boy swung away angrily. He slammed the door of his truck. It was one of those outsize pickup trucks, with big, thick tires. Some sort of machinery in the back. He burned rubber leaving that parking lot. But that wasn't all that was unusual. Jerry Dawson looked as if he'd seen a ghost. I waved to him, since he'd noticed me watching. But he didn't speak or wave back. He just walked off to his car."

"And he didn't bring the matter up to you later?"

"There was no later," Shumate said. "In two days' time, he was dead."

"No idea who the bearded kid was?"

"Dawson's business is renting and leasing film equipment. You

25

know that, I suppose. Quite often Christian filmmakers come to him. He's known for giving them discounts. Since this young fellow sat through the service, I thought his connection to Jerry might be that. He could have been an actor." Shumate shrugged. "Director? I don't know. It's hard to judge people by their appearance anymore."

"His partner might know." Dave stood up. "Thanks for your time." Shumate rose and they shook hands. Dave went to the door, opened it, and turned back. "One more thing. Did he make any extra donations lately?"

"No." Shumate cocked an eyebrow. "Why do you ask?"

"In the last two months, his bank records show he wrote a check for seven hundred dollars and another for three hundred fifty. Not part of his banking pattern."

Shumate scratched an ear. "I don't know," he said.

4

Dave parked in a lot with the laughable name Security half a block below Hollywood Boulevard. Smells of onion, garlic, Parmesan, were thick in the hot air because the kitchen door of Romano's stood open. The old brick had been painted white. Iron barred the windows. He walked out the alley to the street front where the windows had cute green shutters and boxes of geraniums. He paused under a striped sidewalk canopy, thought about a drink, changed his mind. He passed a house-plant boutique, a jazz club with black shutters, a staircase door marked with the names of dentists, a place that hired out tuxedos, and came to the wide plate-glass front of SUPERSTAR RENTALS CINE & SOUND.

Inside, red camera cranes reached for a ceiling hung with spot-lights large and small, round and square. Dollies squatted on thick wheels on a broad floor of vinyl tiles. Microphone booms glittered. There were movieolas, tape recorders, portable and immovable; there was equipment he couldn't put a name to. Cables and cords snaked underfoot. Long-haired youths in bib overalls and straggly moustaches explored the chrome-plated undergrowth. A pale girl in a wrinkled floor-length dress and sandals clutched a clipboard and checked items off a list with a felt pen. All of them whined and neffed at each other and at a resigned, rumpled, obliging bald man who led them to this corner and that, and kept rummaging out for them this scruffy substitute, that battered one. Dave asked him:

"Jack Fullbright?"

"Office," the bald man said, and jerked a thumb at a door beyond a glass counter filled with lenses and microphones on velvet. To reach the door, Dave had to step over a stack of empty thirty-five-millimeter reels. Then he was in a long room where more equipment stood around under weak fluorescent light gathering dust, or lay on steel shelves gathering dust. The aisle between the shelves was made narrow by strapped black wooden cases made for toting film onto and off of jets. Stickers on the boxes showed they'd been to Japan, India, and Beirut, to Spain and Iraq and Yugoslavia. Stacks of film cans also narrowed the aisle, and stacks of brown fiberboard boxes for mailing film reels.

At the end of the aisle a glass box of light was labeled OFFICE. He opened the door and typewriter chatter met him. A young woman who looked like most of the young women on the fronts of magazines these days stopped typing and gave him a smile that by the tiny lines it made in her sun-gilt skin said she wasn't going to be young a lot longer. The wrinkles in the J. C. Penney cheap-rack granny dress of the girl out front had come from sleeping in it. The wrinkles in the loose, unbleached cotton top this young woman wore had cost her the way the trendiest fashions always cost. Her hair was an artfully uncombed tumble of frizz. It was the color of the lenses of her big glasses—amber. Except that in the lenses, the amber turned smoky toward the top. Her voice was warm and jaunty.

"You don't want to rent anything," she said. "You've got every-thing—right?"

"I'm missing facts." Dave laid a card in front of her. "I need to see Jack Fullbright, please."

28

She read the card and her face straightened. She looked up gravely. "About poor Jerry? There's nothing wrong with his life insurance, is there? There couldn't be. I paid his premiums. The bills came here. I paid them with the rest."

"It's not that," Dave said. "It's his death that's got something wrong with it."

"Everything," she said. "He was a fine man."

"His personal accounts came here," Dave said. "You paid all his bills for him—household, and so on?"

"That's right." She tilted her head, frowning. "I don't understand, do I? I mean, it says here you're an investigator. Death claims. What does that mean?"

"Nothing, if you go out quietly in your bed," Dave said. "If you end up the way poor Jerry did, somebody like me comes around to look into why and how. Is Jack Fullbright in, please?"

"Oh, I'm sorry." She glanced at the telephone on her desk. "He's on overseas with London. A shipment got lost. A crew on their way to the north of Norway for a documentary about Lapps or reindeer or moss or something. What do you bet the equipment's in Rio? Luckily, we didn't ship it—they did. Now they want replacements by air freight—at no extra charge."

Dave looked at the glowing button on the phone. "How long can it take?"

"Till Jack wins," she said. "Look—the police already investigated. That lovely tough man with the big shoulders and the broken nose. Lieutenant what?"

"Barker," Dave said. "Ken Barker."

"He seemed to know his job," she said. "Do you always go around checking up on him?"

"He's overworked," Dave said. "He can give any one case only so much time. Los Angeles is big on people killing each other. Happens every day. Sometimes twice. He has to keep moving on to the next one. I don't." Dave glanced behind him. Against a wall of combed plywood, tacked with typed price lists and with calendars big on the phone numbers of sales representatives and freight haulers and small on dates, stood two chairs with split Naugahyde seats. They were heaped with *American Cinematographer* and *Stereo Review* magazines. "Which means I can wait." He set one of the stacks on the floor, sat down, lit a cigarette with a slim steel lighter, and smiled at her. "All right with you?"

"Maybe I can help," she said. "I hope I don't look it, but I'm the man of all work."

"I've been to his bank," Dave said. "The computer printouts puzzle me. I need to see his canceled checks."

"Oh." She gave a little doubtful shake to her head. "I guess I couldn't authorize that, could I?"

"Who is Mrs. Dawson's doctor?" Dave said.

"Dr. Spiegelberg. Irwin. Out near USC."

"She didn't change lately? To a Dr. Encey, out near UCLA?"

She blinked surprise. "Not that I know of. Maybe the bill just hasn't come yet. Did you ask her?"

"I don't believe her," Dave said.

"Oh, my!" Her eyebrows went up. "What kind of nasty, suspicious mind have we here? Not believe Mildred Dawson?"

Dave looked for an ashtray. "When she tells me he gave her a prescription for birth-control pills?"

"Ha!" She had a fine big laugh. "You're kidding. Just flick the ashes on the floor. It's fireproof."

"Where did he keep the girl friend?" Dave asked.

"Girl—" She looked genuinely shocked. "Oh, no, my dear, gorgeous Mr."—she peered through the amber lenses at his card—"Brandstetter, baby. Absolutely not. Never in a million years, love."

Dave shrugged. "His wife's half paralyzed. She's a lot older than he was."

"You don't know Jerry Dawson. There was an obsessively religious man. I'm not talking about Sunday. I'm talking about Monday, Tuesday, Wednesday, Thursday, Friday, Saturday, *and*

Sunday. You better believe it. As for sex—the subject just plain didn't exist." She gave a crooked little remembering smile. "I mean, there was a man who could genuinely blush when a woman said 'damn' in his presence. Definitely up-tight aw-shucks down-home." She gave a little ironic laugh. "A girl friend! Wonderful."

"Who?" A fortyish man who looked harried came out of an inner office. He baked himself a lot by swimming pools. His shirt was open to the navel on a body he plainly worked hard to keep looking young, flat-bellied, chisel-chested. He wore tight linen slacks. A little silver chain circled a throat not quite but almost stringy. He had a blond frontier moustache and blow-dryer hair that looked as if he'd been running his fingers through it. He came to a stop and looked at Dave through big silver-rim dark glasses. "Who are you? I'm Jack Fullbright." He came on, holding out a brown, long-fingered hand.

"Brandstetter." Dave got up and took the hand. It was sweaty but the grip was firm. Fullbright's smile showed big white teeth too even not to have been capped. "I'm an investigator for Gerald Dawson's insurance company. I've got a few questions. Can you give me a little time?"

"Sure, sure." Fullbright tilted his head at the office door. "Go right in. Pour yourself a drink. I'll be right there." He bent over the poodle-haired girl, spreading rumpled carbon copies of shipping manifests on her desk. "We'll split the air fare. This is what they need, absolute minimum. Get it off by Emery as soon as Rog can collect and pack it, right? I'll talk to him about the overtime—don't worry. Meantime, get SeaLanes to put out a tracer from San Pedro. They're already doing that from Southampton. Got it?"

"You're going to split the charges?"

"Not till SeaLanes makes it up to us. Good baby." He came into a room that didn't look as if it bore any relation to the girl's office. There was a lot of real paneling and genuine cowhide. Where there was no sense in there being a window, since outside were only trash cans and parking lots, stood an eighteenth-century Japanese fold-

31

ing screen—or a good reproduction. People in small boats admiring a moon above piny mountains. The bar that Fullbright went behind wasn't Formica—it was honest-to-God teak. "Hey, sorry to keep you waiting." He rattled Swedish crystal and a bottle of Schweppes from a refrigerator he had to stoop to. Ice cubes fell out of his hands into the glasses as in a conjuring trick. He waved a green bottle. Tanqueray. "Gin and tonic all right with you? I mean, I've got Heineken's here."

"Gin and tonic is fine," Dave said. "Thanks."

Fullbright poured. "What's wrong about Jerry? I thought the police had the case taped. He tried to put a local, friendly pornographer out of business, and the local friendly put him out of business instead. No?"

"You don't sound moved," Dave said.

"He knew this operation." Fullbright dropped sprigs of mint on top of the ice and bubbles in the glasses. "He handled money well." Fullbright came from behind the bar, handed a glass to Dave, and sat down at his desk. "But he was a sanctimonious pain in the ass."

"His wife and your secretary tell me his canceled checks are here," Dave said. "Can I see them? He wrote a couple in the last few weeks that need explaining."

"Why? To whom?" Fullbright looked wary.

"To me. Nobody knows where he was that night. That bothers me. I think something was going on in his life besides this business, that church, and his family."

"He was out with his 'Keep Our City Clean for Christ' squad." Fullbright shrugged disgust and drank. "Ripping up the seats of X-rated movie houses and castrating faggots. Saving our children, as the orange-juice lady says."

"I don't think so," Dave said. "The checks?"

"Have you got the right?" Fullbright set down his drink and reached for his phone. "I better check with our lawyer."

"As long as I go on thinking," Dave said, "that Lon Tooker

32

didn't kill Gerald Dawson but that maybe Mildred did, or Bucky, Sequoia Life and Indemnity is going to keep the fifty thousand dollars Dawson meant for them to have. Have you got something against them?"

Fullbright was staring. "Mildred? Bucky? You think they killed him?"

"For reasons that would make you laugh or cry if I named them to you," Dave said. "Let's clear up my sordid imaginings, shall we? Show me the checks."

Fullbright's hand was on the phone but his suntan had turned a little yellow. He let the phone go and stood up. "Come on," he said without expression, and went out of the office, across the plywood room where the secretary was pointing out things on the shipping manifests to the bald man, and into another office where a big film poster featuring a hilltop crucifixion against a stormy sky was framed above a desk coated with dust. Fullbright pulled open the top drawer of a green metal file cabinet. "In here." He gave Dave a sour glance and started out of the room. "Help yourself."

"Leave the door open," Dave said.

Fullbright left the door open. He didn't go back to his office. He went with the bald man into the storeroom.

The checks were in the envelopes the bank had mailed them in. The bundles for each month were wrapped in blue and white statement sheets. The one for seven hundred dollars and the one for three hundred fifty were both written to a Sylvia Katzman. The rubber stamps on the back in red said hers was a Proctor Bank account, Westwood branch. Dave put the checks back and shut the file drawer.

"Thanks," he said to the secretary.

She was talking into her phone. She waved a ball-point pen at him without looking up.

In the storeroom, the bald man was on his knees, working up a sweat, grappling with some heavy piece of equipment on a lower shelf. Fullbright stood over him, reading the crumpled manifest in his hand. Dave asked him:

"Did Dawson have a young customer with a black beard who drove a big pickup truck, machinery in the back?"

"If he did," Fullbright grunted, "I never saw him."

"Thanks," Dave said.

5

At the dark little bar, he used Max Romano's phone to reach Mel Fleischer at Proctor Bank headquarters. And to find Amanda where he feared he'd find her, moping around that big, beautiful, blank house in Beverly Glen, needing somebody to get her off dead center. He'd failed before. This time she said she'd come. She came. She stood blinded in the shadowy restaurant after the savagery of the street glare, swaying a little, afraid to take a step. She too wore one of those wrinkled, blowsy, loose-woven cotton tops over knickers and knee boots. From her shoulder hung a straw bag that matched the floppy sun hat on her dark, wing-smooth hair. Max, bald and pudgy, arm loaded with menus, waddled to her and spoke to her, probably gentle words about Carl Brandstetter's death. And she saw Dave and came on, doing her best to smile. It was going to take more practice. Dave got off his stool to move the next one for her.

"You look great," he said.

"I feel forlorn," she said. "I hate it when people go away and don't come back." The bartender raised eyebrows at her and she nodded at Dave's drink. "But what right have I got to mourn to you? I have only a year's worth of memories to ache over. You've got a lifetime's."

"You couldn't help it," he said. "Nobody could. It was going to happen and it happened. You're young. Start over."

"I keep walking in circles," she said, "like something sad in a zoo. Only sadder."

"No. You've got the key. Open the cage. Go."

"Where?" Bleakly she rummaged in the straw bag. Cigarettes came out, the thin, long, brown kind. She set one in her mouth and pushed the pack at Dave. He took one and lit hers and his with the thin steel lighter. "At least when I'm home, I see him, I hear him. This room, that room, out by the pool. I hear that laugh of his. He makes a loud ghost."

"You can turn into a ghost yourself that way," Dave said. He watched the bartender set a glass in front of her. He took the ticket. "I know. I went through it a couple of years ago. Till I got out of the house we'd shared, I couldn't function. Even after I found somebody alive and he came in and rattled around in the kitchen and slept in the bed with me, it was no good."

"Doug?" she said. And answered her own question with a nod. "Yes, Doug. And now he never knows where you are when I ring you up." She tasted the drink.

"He never knew where I was before," Dave said.

"You're breaking up," she said. "And you're 'no longer with us' when I call your office at Medallion."

"I got out of there before they threw me out," he said. "With no time to spare. Walking through that tenth floor the day after he died was like swimming through a school of great white sharks. Vice presidents."

She peered at him. "You're joking. Aren't you? I mean, why? Why would they throw you out?"

"Bad employment risk." He tilted up his glass and let the ice rattle against his mouth. "Untrustworthy."

"But you were there for years!" she protested.

"Forever," he said. "Shall we eat?"

In drum chairs upholstered in black crushed velvet at a table where a candle flickered in a tubby amber chimney, she laid down the big, floppy menu. "Don't you own stock? I thought Carl said—"

"Enough so I won't starve," he said, "but not fifty-one percent." He put on shell-rim half-moon glasses to read the menu and wondered if the cold salmon was fresh. "Not enough to control policy. Carl had the fifty-one percent. But it won't stay in a block. Not now. The widows will get it. Sorry."

"Not this one," she said. "A house worth conservatively a quarter of a million dollars, and two expensive automobiles. One. The Bentley was totaled. He didn't leave them the shares."

"They'll get them in court," Dave said. "That's the kind of lady he married. Present company excepted. And Lisa, possibly. And probably Helena—she already owns two hundred racehorses and half Ventura County." He laid aside the menu, took off the reading glasses, and tucked them into his pocket. "The stuffed flounder is reliable."

"I'll have the stuffed flounder, then," she said. "You come here a lot, don't you?"

"Since Max had a full head of hair," Dave said. "Nineteen forty-eight. That would be well before you were born." He looked around. "Maybe I'll stop, now. One ghost too many, I think."

"We were here one night with that police lieutenant. Mr. Barker. He said you were the best in the business. How could they fire you?"

"He's a friend of mine," Dave said.

"Carl said so too." She swallowed some of her drink. "And I've read clippings. *Newsweek. The New York Times Magazine. People.*"

"Dear God," Dave said. "Did he keep clippings? The sentimental old bastard. I never knew that."

"He thought the world of you," she said.

"Please stop," he said. And Max touched his shoulder and set a French boudoir telephone on the table and crouched with a grunt to plug it in. Dave picked up the receiver, looking *excuse me* at Amanda. In his ear, Mel Fleischer said, "Sylvia Katzman lives in one of thirty-eight units she owns up above the Sunset Strip." He read off the address. "How's Doug? Gallery beginning to pay its way?" Doug sold pictures, sculpture, and pottery on Robertson where everyone else sold antiques. Mel Fleischer collected California painters of the twenties and thirties. He owned more Millard Sheets pictures than anyone else. Mel said, "Has he tracked down that Redmond for me, yet? It's a grisaille of eucalyptus trees by a pond. Some detective-story writer owned it who died. Is the will out of probate yet?"

"You've got me," Dave said. "Doug doesn't talk to me a whole hell of a lot. He talks French to a Polynesian princess called Christian Jacques who runs a restaurant across from the gallery. If you can't reach him at home, try the Bamboo Raft."

"Oh, is that how it is?" Mel said. "Listen, I was so sorry to hear about your father."

"Thanks," Dave said. "Look, I want to buy you dinner for this. Tonight? Tomorrow?"

"Tomorrow. And can it be for two?" Mel asked. "And Japanese? I mean, who can stand all that vinegar and raw fish? But there's this adorable boy who can't seem to stop creeping into my rickety old couch of pain. And wherever I go, I glance over my stooped and aged shoulder, and there he is, with longing in his almond eyes. Of course, I'm going to wake up and it will all be a dream. He's all of twenty-two. Can you feature it?"

"Bring him along," Dave said.

"He wears happy coats," Mel said. "You know, the short ones that come about to here? 'Happy' is hardly the word. Would you accept 'hysterical'?"

"In your case, yes," Dave said. "Make it Noguchi's on Sawtelle

Boulevard. That's just above Venice. About eight o'clock? And, hey—thanks for Sylvia Katzman."

"I have a feeling she won't thank me," Mel said.

"I won't mention your name," Dave said. "That way, she can't send you poison-pen letters from Tehachapi."

"Bless you," Mel said. "See you tomorrow night."

Dave hung up. He said to Amanda, "Clippings don't mean a damn to vice presidents. They can't read."

"What you're saying is," she said, "that they always wanted you out, but they couldn't do anything about it while Carl was alive."

"He warned me," Dave said. "There's an annual prize given to the biggest fag-haters. The front-runners are always the same—police departments large and small; governments federal, state, and local; the Florida orange-juice crowd; the army, navy, and marines; homosexuals themselves; and insurance companies. Only the last two are not sucker bets. And the insurance companies always win. Everything."

"Like the Las Vegas casinos?" she said.

"Penny-ante stuff," Dave said. "The casinos have to play fair. Who ever heard of an insurance company playing fair? When they don't like the odds, they cancel out."

"You're strange." She blinked through the cigarette smoke that curled lazily around the candle chimney. "Why did you stay in the business if you hate it so? Because of Carl? It was all right if it was him doing it?"

"My part was to play straight in a vicious game," he said. "I liked it. I still do. That's why I'm not quitting. I'm one of the lucky people getting paid to do what I love to do. Almost no one manages that in this life. Oh, I'd rather have written a good string quartet. I couldn't write even a bad string quartet."

A waiter in a black velvet jacket took their orders.

"I'm not good at anything," Amanda said.

"You decorated that house," Dave said. "They had it in *Home* magazine. Why don't you set up shop on Rodeo? Better still why don't you decorate my new place for me? As of day before yesterday, it's all mine, the bank says."

"You make me dizzy," she said.

"Not so dizzy as walking around in circles feeling sorry for yourself," Dave said. "We'll go there after lunch. All right? Get ready for a challenge."

"You're working," she said. "You mustn't feel you have to give me occupational therapy."

"Gerald Dawson isn't going to get any deader," Dave said. "And his wife and son aren't going to run away. If I were them I would but they won't."

"What kind of place have you found?" she asked.

"I think the former owner was a wolf in a grandmother's nightcap," Dave said.

He took three wrong turnings up shaggy Laurel Canyon before he found the right one. He'd only been twice before. And his mind was on Jack Fullbright. When Dave had gone back out to the sizzling parking lot, he'd seen Fullbright loading a cardboard carton full of files into the hatchback of a flame-painted Datsun 260Z. What for? Was it regular? Fullbright's clothes, suntan, manner, car, didn't belong to the image of a man who took the office home with him. Didn't the police case file on the Dawson murder say Fullbright lived on a power launch at the marina? But how had Dave put the wind up him? By asking to see into the files? Which meant to Fullbright he might ask again? So Fullbright removed what he didn't want seen? What? Why?

The road was called Horseshoe Canyon and it was steep and only one car wide, and the blacktop was gray with age and had potholes that were almost craters. The Electra lurched and scraped bottom, climbing. Back of him, he saw in his mirrors Amanda's Bugatti managing the climb nimbly as a spider. The Electra was so long it was hard to get it to turn in at the wrecked driveway that dropped down to the house, which crouched, all weathered brown shingles, under ragged pines and eucalyptus. Actually it was three buildings joined by roofs. He got out of the Electra. Amanda got out of the Bugatti and said:

"Yes, well—you'll want gardeners right away, won't you?" She crunched across shed needles, leaves, peeled bark. "French doors all the way across. That's nice."

"You ain't seen nothin' yet," Dave said, and led her around to the courtyard, where a wide-spreading old live oak sheltered paving whose square red tiles had sunk and tilted and made treacherous footing. A broad, heavy door, squared off in glass panes, opened onto a single wood-walled room crossed by big beams under a pitched roof. "Thirty-six feet by twenty-two feet. How about that?"

"It's glorious," she said. But she frowned at the fieldstone fireplace at the end. "That's a bit stingy, isn't it? And the materials are wrong. And it's the wrong shape. What do you say to something about this wide"—she stretched her arms—"with a raised hearth? Secondhand brick, no?"

"I don't have to say anything," Dave said. "You say."

She cocked her head at him, and her little smile said she couldn't quite believe her luck. She shrugged, took off the hat, and pirouetted slowly, looking the room over. "It's so California," she said. She rubbed a circle in the dust of a windowpane to see out. She said, "You don't want to cut all those marvelous trees. They're so right for the place. It's John Muir, isn't it, John Burroughs, Joaquin Miller?"

"With smog," he said.

She ignored that, took steps backward, frowning up, nibbling her lip. "But they do make it dark. What do you say to clerestory windows above the French doors?"

"Raise the roof, kid," he said. "The shop on Rodeo was a good idea. You spend other people's money with grace and abandon. They'll love you in Beverly Hills."

She blinked at him. "Those tainted shares?"

"Hey," he said. "Do it. Start today. Only first, come look at the cookhouse."

But an engine roared outside. Amanda turned again to peer through the glass. "You've got visitors," she said.

They went back out to the cars. A tow truck tilted backward down off the potholed trail. A leathery man in greasy coveralls was squatting to fasten the winch hook under the back of the Electra. When he saw Dave, he took a folded paper out of his breast pocket and handed it to him. "Brandstetter?" he said.

"Right. But I didn't call you."

"It's Medallion Life Insurance." The voice belonged to a boy with yellow rag-doll hair in the cab of the wrecker. "It's a company car. You don't work for them anymore. They want their car back."

Amanda stared at Dave. He grinned.

"You're not going to believe this," he said, "but I honest to Christ forgot. This is the twelfth or thirteenth one. It got to be a habit. I haven't driven a car that belonged to me in my entire life." He laughed and lifted a hand to the tow-truck man. "Take her away, friend."

"You want to get anything out of it?" the man said.

"No, but you want the keys, right?" Dave handed them to him. "There's a ball-point pen and a pad of paper with nothing on it in the glove compartment. A rag to wipe the windshield. And an operator's manual. Medallion is welcome to them."

"But what will you do?" Amanda cried.

"Get you to drive me down out of here," Dave said. "Once you've got your list of things to do to the house ready. Then you can help me pick a car I can get into this driveway."

6

The Triumph kept trying to run out from under him. His foot was going to have to learn new gentleness or he would end up on the moon. He left it in a parking lot bulldozed out of hillside back of a row of stucco store buildings, record shops, places to eat and drink, second floors filled with talent agencies and ex-UCLA film students claiming to be producers. The parking lot was filled with vans and Porsches and Lotuses, paid for by dreary fathers in Des Moines and Kansas City with more love or desperation than common sense. It was a quiet, empty time on the sidewalk that passed the shops. A black youth sat on a curb, elbows on knees, hands clutching his head, talking softly to himself. A girl in a T-shirt stenciled COWGIRLS NEED LOVE TOO went past with a canvas guitar case. She wore denim short shorts and tooled boots. A trio of twelve-year-olds of one sex or another came out of a shop, each carrying a *Grease* album, and wobbled away down the sidewalk on ten-speed bicycles.

Nobody much was in the drugstore. There were long shiny aisles of toys and cosmetics, headache remedies and cold medicines, paperback books and bath towels, drinking glasses and electric can openers. A box of wax crayons lay in the aisle he took, broken open, strewn. With a red one a little fist had traced FUK on the glossy floor covering. Bernard Shaw would have liked the spelling. Dave crouched and dropped the crayons back into the box, shut the box, laid it back with the dozen yellow-orange boxes just like it.

The next section of the aisle was lined on one side with rakes, hoes, trowels, with flower pots plain and glazed, with bright little growing plants in green metal racks, and on the other with bags of plant food and fertilizer and peat moss. Motor-oil cans were stacked at the end of the aisle. And he was facing a white counter with a sign above it in gold cutout letters—PRESCRIPTIONS. A gray-haired man bent his head over something beyond glass panes. Dave tapped a bell on the counter and the man came out in a white jacket with a yellow SMILE button pinned to it. He was Japanese, with baggy eyes and horn-rim glasses. They were bifocals, and he tilted his head back to read the license Dave showed him.

Dave said, "I'm investigating the death of Gerald Dawson. For Sequoia, the company that insured his life. He picked up a prescription in here." Dave named the date.

"I can't reveal anything about prescriptions." The pharmacist handed back Dave's wallet. "You know that."

"You don't have to. It was for birth-control pills. Dawson picked it up for his wife. All I want to know is, did you ever see his wife?"

"Hundreds of people get prescriptions filled here," the pharmacist said. "You said he picked it up. You want to know what his wife looked like. Does that make sense to you? That doesn't make sense to me."

A young man who had to be the pharmacist's son came rattling down a set of steps at the back of the glassed-in room. He came out to the counter with a carton marked UPJOHN in his hands. "I remember him," he told Dave, "because the next morning they had it on TV he was murdered."

"I'm making up a prescription," his father said, and went back to bend his head over his work again.

"They had his picture." The boy worked the latch of a white gate that broke the counter and came out with the box. He set it on the floor, tore it open, began taking bottles out of it and arranging them on a low shelf. "It said he was a churchgoer, a pillar of his church, right?"

"That's the man," Dave said.

"Maybe," the boy said. "But not his wife. No way."

"A woman about sixty," Dave said. "Paralyzed on one side. Drags her foot."

"That's what's wrong," the pharmacist's son said. "She's about fifteen years old. And I mean, she is wild. Did you see the ice-cream counter? Up front by the check stands? You know what she made him do while he waited to get the prescription, right here where you're standing? She made him buy her three ice-cream cones. At once. And there's a record counter over there." He pointed. "There's nothing to play them on. I mean, they're junk. Boxcar-sale stuff. If you listened to them you wouldn't buy them, okay? So what does she do? She goes to the kiddies' toys. And there's these little ten-dollar players, plastic, made to look like bugs and panda bears and that. And she takes and finds a floor plug in the lamps and she sits down and plays the record. Loud? I mean, loud-loud! And the poor man is standing here turning redder and redder, right? And she's sitting there on the floor in her little shorts and tank top and licking first one flavor ice-cream cone and then another flavor and then another one and dripping it all over the rug, right? I remember her."

"Who's Doctor Encey?" Dave asked.

"One of the happiness boys," the pharmacist's son said. "The tall glass building two blocks thataway."

"You mean he sells prescriptions," Dave said.

"They're usually to put actors to sleep or to wake writers up or keep directors calm. Or people who call themselves those things. But they can be almost anything."

"You fill the prescriptions?" Dave asked.

"That's what we're here for," the boy said. He put the last bottle on the shelf, poked the flaps of the empty carton down into it, and stood up. "Encey's still got his license. It's no secret what he's doing. Nobody in charge seems to want to stop him. What did Dawson get that night? Birth-control pills? That's not such a big deal."

"You're sure the girl was with him?" Dave said.

"They were in together before. She points. 'Buy me this, buy me that.' He falls all over himself to buy it. She's not very bright. I mean"—he edged past Dave with the empty carton, back behind the counter, clicking the lock shut on the white gate—"she used poor English. I think she's a high-school dropout, one of those runaways. 'I'm going to be in the movies, I'm going to be on TV,' you know? Come to Hollywood. I don't know where a man like that found her. I mean—he looked like what they said he was on the news—somebody who passes the collection plate in church Sunday mornings. Typecasting."

"She impressed you," Dave said. "Is she pretty?"

"Too young. Flat-chested, hips like a Little League pitcher." He frowned to himself, blinking. "I don't know. There's hundreds of them along this street. But, yeah—she was different. They've all got Farrah Fawcett hair, you know? Looks like they borrowed it?"

"Blond and abundant," Dave said.

"Howard?" the gray-haired man called.

"Have you seen her in the last week?" Dave asked.

"I don't think so," the boy said. "Excuse me?"

Outside in the heat, the black boy had got up off the curb and was acting. He was waving clenched fists, popping his eyes, and mouthing angry words without sound. Two sweat-shiny college boys jogged past in red track shorts. They didn't even turn their heads. The black boy seemed to be looking at Dave but he wasn't. What he saw was inside his skull. A shiny green moped buzzed around the corner. A girl in a bikini rode it. Flat-chested. Quantities of yellow hair. Dark glasses. Had Jerry Dawson bought her a motorbike? It purred on past.

No one had slashed the cloth top of the Triumph. It whipped out of the parking lot. It seemed to have only two speeds—motionless and breakneck. As he steered it out Sunset, the speedometer kept jumping from zero to sixty. The street off the Strip where Sylvia Katzman's sand-color boxes of apartment units climbed the hill rose in sharp bends. The Triumph zipped up them with brisk little shrieks from the new tires. The address was in big wooden cutout numbers that stuck out on tin struts from the stucco. Dave ducked the car under the place and into a tenant's empty parking slot. The door at the top of inside stairs was locked. He went up the ramp to the sidewalk and climbed for the front doors among plantings. He'd warned her by phone from the expensive cowhide-smelling Jaguar-Triumph agency that he was coming, and she was waiting for him in the lobby in a green-and-yellow striped tank top and yellow shorts, harlequin glasses set with rhinestones, and yellow platform sandals. Her hair was brassy piled-up ringlets. She was five feet tall and twenty pounds overweight. She unlocked the glass door for him.

"I don't understand what it's about," she said. "Insurance, did you say? A tenant of mine?"

"Gerald Dawson. I don't know whether he was a tenant or not. I only know he made out two checks to you in the past eight weeks."

"He didn't live here," she said. "It was for his daughter. Charleen. She'd married somebody and they split up and her mother wouldn't have her back and her father felt different about it and he got this place for her. On the quiet, you understand. Is there something wrong or something?"

47

"He's dead," Dave said. "Is his daughter here?"

"Oh, dear," she said. "Oh, that's too bad. The poor man. He wasn't even old. What happened?"

"Somebody broke his neck on a dark street," Dave said. "Or that's how it looks."

"Listen," she said, "it happens every day. What do you think I pay for security for around here? I light the front of this place like a—you should excuse the expression—Christmas tree. Do you know what's down there? On that Sunset Strip? People out of a nightmare, that's what. I keep that garage lighted. I have a man down there at night in a uniform with a gun. He'd probably shoot himself in the foot if he had to use it, but maybe he'll scare the muggers and the rapists, you know? What can you do?"

"What about Dawson's daughter?" Dave asked.

"She must be on a trip," Sylvia Katzman said. "I haven't seen her for days."

"It's a big place," Dave said. "You could have missed her. You don't play *concierge*, do you?"

"I play pan," she said, "three nights a week. If you mean, do I watch the tenants going in and out—no, of course not. Everybody has their own life. They're entitled to be free. This isn't Europe, thank God. This isn't Russia. Where they go and when they come back is their business."

"What's her apartment number?" Dave asked.

"Thirty-six. On the third level. With a view."

"Who came to see her?" Dave asked. "Anybody besides Gerald Dawson? Part of your security system involves tenants having to come down here in person to let their visitors in, right?"

"Unless they lend their key," she said. "They're not supposed to, but who can predict what people will do? Could I see your identification?"

He let his wallet fall open so she could read his investigator's license. "She ought to be told her father is dead," he said. "The funeral is tomorrow. No one else in the family knew she was here."

"She won't go to the funeral," Sylvia Katzman said. "She won't even care that he's dead. Except he won't be here to pay her rent anymore. He was very good to her, and she treated him like dirt. Listen, mothers know girls. Fathers can be fooled. Her mother was right."

Somewhere distant a telephone rang. Sylvia Katzman waggled pudgy, ringed fingers toward carpeted stairs. "Go, maybe she's home." She hurried off in the direction of the ringing phone, buttocks wobbling inside the tight shorts. "You're a nice man to come and tell her. But you're wasting your—" A door closed, cutting off the last word. If with Sylvia Katzman there ever was a last word.

Dave climbed in air-conditioned silence to the third level and went along a gallery past five glass fronts to the glass front of thirty-six. She was right. The view was good. It would be better without the brown haze. But below, Los Angeles sloped off for miles toward the sea. On a clear night there would be a carpet of lights, on a clear day treetops. The curtains were drawn on thirty-six. He pressed a button. A buzzer went off inside but no one came to the door. Somebody had scraped with a thumbnail at a United Fund Drive sticker inside the glass. The traffic down on Sunset made surf noises. A blue jay squawked. Dave poked the buzzer again. Again no one came. He snapped open a leather key case and slipped a small blade into the lock. It turned.

The walls were bare and painted melon color. He stood on brown shag carpet. Brown velour couches made an open-sided square around a coffee table where flowers were dead in a brown pottery bowl. He smelled decayed food. Two TV dinners in aluminum trays lay on a brown Formica counter with melon-color stools. Mold grew on the food, and soft drinks evaporated in glasses. Beside an incongruously clean stainless steel sink were stacked unwashed dishes. When he opened doors under the sink, soft drink cans, Colonel Sanders boxes, taco wrappers tumbled onto a spotlessly clean, glossily waxed floor. Incongruous again. He opened the window over the sink to let the garbage smell out if it would go. Almost near enough the window to reach out and touch, an embankment, propped at its foot by cement blocks, rose very steeply twelve, fifteen feet to a curved street. On the near side of the street, a chain-link fence had been cut into at the bottom, the corners of the cut folded back. The refrigerator hummed.

In the bedroom, the piece of furniture meant to be slept on was round. The sheets were satin or some wonders-of-modern-science substitute. They were melon-color and half off the bed that looked as if wrestling had taken place there. A pillow half out of its melon satin cover lay in a corner. He opened closet doors that ran on rollers. Not much hung there, and what did smelled of stale sweat. Dresser drawers held blue jeans and T-shirts and pullover sweaters with the kind of turtleneck that droops. There were pantyhose, little clean underpants, little clean socks. He shut the drawers. In the bathroom, the medicine chest held aspirin, cold medicine, deodorant, toothpaste, toothbrush, disposable razor. Hair had been cut in here. Dark tufts lay in corners of the coral tile floor. It clogged the basin drain.

He went back into the bedroom and frowned around at it. What was missing was a jacket to keep her warm nights. The closet had showed him caps, hats, a couple of flimsy scarves and a tumble of shoes. He blinked. A poster was Scotch-taped to the wall over the bed. A naked young man knelt, face pressed into the belly of a standing girl whose head was thrown back, lips parted, eyes closed. She was naked too. His hands gripped her buttocks. The background was black. The lettering was red. ALL THE WAY DOWN. That was at the top. At the foot was A SPENCE ODUM PRODUCTION. The girl had big breasts and didn't appear to be blond.

Out in the room with the view, he looked again at the glasses on the breakfast bar. Each of the abandoned soft drinks had a plastic swizzle stick angling down into it. One was a sickly yellow, the other a sickly blue. He bent close but the light was bad. He found a switch and bulbs went on inside brown, hard-finish lamp shades over pottery bases around the room. They gave feeble light but it was enough. Lettering was stamped into the sticks. He put on his glasses and bent close again, trying not to breathe the stink of the decayed food. The lettering read THE STRIP JOINT and gave an address on Sunset.

He tucked his glasses away, rubbed at the aluminum plate around the door lock with a handkerchief, and rolled the door shut with the handkerchief covering his fingers. The lock clicked. He pushed the handkerchief away in a pocket and pressed the button at thirty-five. No one came. No one came when he pressed the other buttons down the line. All the units on this level watched the soiled and poisonous air blind, deaf, and lifeless. It didn't matter. He already had too many answers. What he needed now were the questions to go with them.

7

CINZANO was stenciled large on the red-and-blue umbrellas over the tables in front of the Strip Joint. At the tables, youngsters in bikinis and surfer trunks, ragged straw hats and armless shirts, breathed the exhaust fumes of the close-packed homebound traffic on the street, and washed down avocado-burgers with Cokes, Seven-Ups, Perrier water. Scuba-diving goggles set in black rubber rested on top of the long wet golden hair of a suntanned youth. Edging between the crowded tables, Dave stumbled over swim fins. There was the cocoa-butter smell of Skol.

Inside, the smell was of bourbon and smoke—not all of it tobacco smoke. The lights, if there were any, hadn't been turned on. If you wanted to see, you saw by what filtered in from the dying day outside through bamboo-blinded plate glass. The crowd in here appeared older, and Peter Frampton wasn't blaring from loudspeakers as he was outside. Dave sat on a bamboo stool beside a plump, chattering man in a checked linen jacket, and told a vague shape in skin-tight coveralls behind the bar that he wanted a gin and tonic. In the gloom at the room's end, a pair of angular lads in black, not-very-crisp shirts and jeans was puttering with microphones, amplifiers, speakers, on a small platform. Feedback screamed. Everyone looked at the corner. The feedback stopped. The bartender set the gin and tonic in front of Dave but didn't go away. He stood leaning with his hands on the bar.

"You want something else?"

"What more could I possibly want?"

"It's always something," the bartender said. "What is it this time? Who's supposed to be dealing in here now? Who's supposed to be snorting in the men's room?"

"I'm not a cop," Dave told him.

"You're something like that," the bartender said. He had a drooping, corn-color moustache and his hair was going thin, but his skin had a youthful sheen to it and his eyes were clear and healthy. They blinked, speculative. "Maybe you're a deprogrammer, except I can't smell greed on you. You can't be a private eye. They don't have those anymore. And when they had them, they didn't look like you."

"Insurance," Dave said. "Have you seen a thin girl child named Charleen? Blond, about five-four, no breasts to speak of, no hips to speak of, maybe in company with a small, dark, intense church-deacon type in his forties?"

"The kids can't come inside during the day," the bartender said, "and that's when I work so I wouldn't see a kid." He looked past Dave. He called, "Priss?"

The young woman who came wore the same sort of baby-blue bib coveralls as the bartender, except the legs of hers were cut very short and with little splits at the sides. She had loose poodle hair like the secretary at Superstar Rentals. Her smile was bright, brisk, professional. The bartender asked her about Charleen.

"She came here," Dave said. "She had swizzle sticks with the name of this place on them."

"Oh, honey." The girl laid a hand with open fingers on her forehead. "They come by the gross. Is that all you've got? Haven't you got a picture?"

"They were an odd couple," Dave said. He described Dawson again.

"What's odd?" Priss wagged her head with a wan smile. "Sweetheart, a girl could come here with a two-toed sloth and nobody would notice."

"The kids do come in here at night, right?" Dave said to the bartender. "You've got a band. Not for us tone-deaf old drunks, surely. So they must dance, no?"

"That wall slides back. On the other side. Soft drinks only. Eight-thirty. Also junk food, okay?"

"That all?" Priss wondered.

Dave lifted his glass to her. "Remember me to the two-toed sloths."

She went away. So did the bartender. Dave worked his way through clusters of balding men talking talent, talking albums, talking contracts, to the little platform. One of the angular youths had gone off. The other one sat at the keyboard, fiddling with switches, playing runs. Dave stepped up onto the platform. Drumsticks lay crossed on a snare. He picked one up and tapped a cymbal. The youth at the keyboard turned to him, flinching.

"Mustn't touch," he said.

Dave put the stick down carefully and told him about Charleen and Gerald Dawson.

"He's a bad dancer," the skinny youth said. "The worst she ever brought. But she only brought the other ones once. They liked it. He hated it. It figured she'd bring him back over and over."

"Sensitive to others, was she?" Dave said.

"He was a jerk. He deserved it. What did he need with her? She was like a ten-year-old. No boobs, no nothing. But he fell all over himself. She could make him do anything. And she wasn't even smart."

"You sound like you knew her," Dave said.

His hair was black and lank, lusterless, uncombed. It went inside the greasy collar of his shirt when he shook his head. He ran long, knuckly fingers under it to free it. "You sit up here and run through the same sets night after night it gets mechanical and boring," he said. "So I watch, you know? What you see isn't Aldrich or Coppola or Scorsese, and it's only clips, but I make up the rest of the script. She's this turkey-ranch hick, right? And she runs away from Gobbler Gulch to the bright lights, and the town preacher comes to fetch her and it's Sadie Thompson all over again. You know that old Joan Crawford flick? That was John Huston's father in that, did you know? John Huston is old as God himself. That was a long time ago, man."

"You made this up," Dave said. "But you never talked to her?"

"Did I say that?" The knuckly fingers played a phrase from "The Maid with the Flaxen Hair." The electronic sounds came out tinkling, silvery. "I talked to her. She was a talker. Anybody she could grab. She was going to get into films. She was peddling her scrawny little ass up and down the Strip all night. And the johns she got all told her the same thing. They were agents, directors, producers. They'd get her into films. And she believed them. They told her she had beautiful facial planes, all right?" Woodwinds faked themselves inside the circuitry. What came from under his fingers sounded tender, yearning. It contradicted the sourness of his words.

"What did you tell her?" Dave asked. "That you could get her a recording contract?"

"My sheets needed changing," he said. "My decor is piles of dirty laundry. She liked my cock very much but I don't think my life-style convinced her I had the clout to help her with her career." He snapped off a little what-the-hell laugh but the music kept on sounding sentimental.

"Dawson wasn't an agent, a director, a producer," Dave said. "He couldn't get her into pictures."

"I don't know." The shoulders went up and down without affecting the smooth work the fingers were doing. "He sure as hell didn't look it. Him I'd have figured to be paying the rent or something, you know? But about the time I saw him with her first, a little before, she said she'd made it. She had a part. A big part. She was going to be a movie star. She'd even met the producer."

"Did she name him?" Dave said.

"How could she name him? Somebody drives a new Seville along here waving an open door at the girls on the sidewalk—he's going to give his real name?" The Ravel piece came to an end. He looked at Dave. "Who are you and what do you want with her?"

"You said the man would do anything for her," Dave told him. "I think he died for her. He died, that's for sure. If I can find her, maybe she can tell me why."

"She hasn't been around," the musician said.

"For how long?" Dave said. He named the date of Gerald Dawson's death. "Would that be the last time?"

"You think she's dead?" His skin never saw sunlight. The darkness of his hair and moustache, the intensity of the little light glaring off the sheet music on the instrument, reflecting into his face, made it look like ivory. Now it turned to chalk. "Christ, she was only sixteen."

"Is the date right?" Dave said.

"Yeah. No. I don't know. Who reads calendars all the time? Every night is the same in here." His mouth trembled. He sounded as if he were going to cry. "Jesus. I guess that's right. Ten days ago, right? Yeah, it must have been about that long."

"She hasn't been back to her apartment," Dave said. "Where else would she go?"

"I don't know, man. She slept around, right? For bread. I mean, nobody's ever going to get her into that glass slipper. A pumpkin is always going to be a pumpkin for her. What a dumb, crazy little kid."

"Do you write your own lyrics?" Dave said.

He grinned wanly. "That's a quote from some flick." But the tune under his fingers now was "Pavanne for a Dead Princess," the celesta sound giving it a toy-shop aptness. "Who knows? You could check who's suddenly signed million-dollar contracts and moved into Beverly Hills mansions."

"Million-dollar contracts I don't think she'd get," Dave said. "Did you ever hear of a producer called Odum? Spence Odum?"

"They keep making those pictures about that Little League baseball team. The Bad News Bears. She could be in the next one. *The Bad News Bears Meet the Dirty Old Men?*"

"She didn't tell you this producer who signed her was named Spence Odum?"

"She didn't give me the name," he said. "She stuck out her tongue when I asked her. She flounced away, right? Grammarschool stuff. 'Ask me no questions, I'll tell you no lies.' " He made his voice simpering. His hand flipped switches. Debussy mourned. Then stopped. The cover came down over the keyboards. "I've got to eat."

Dave gave him a card. "If you remember anything about her that you haven't told me, call me, will you?"

The card went into a shirt pocket where there were ball-point pens and cigarettes. The skeletal thighs slid off the high bench. "Later," he said, and dropped off the platform and wove in and out through the knots of talkers, and after a pause to put on dark glasses, out into what was left of the daylight. Dave set down his unfinished drink and followed. Eating still went on. So did Peter Frampton. The temperature had cooled and shirts had come from nowhere to cover the suntan-oiled shoulders. Priss came at him, empty tray at her side.

"Charleen Sims," she said. "A big, dumb kid was here with a picture. Scrawny little blond. In a high-school yearbook from some tacky little town in the boonies. Showing her picture to everybody. Had anybody seen Charleen? I forgot before."

"Now is a good time," Dave said. "What did this big, dumb kid look like? Did he have a name? What was the name on the year-book? What tacky little town in the boonies?"

"You know what you could take him for?" she asked.

"A two-toed sloth?" Dave said.

"Big Foot," she said. "The monster that's supposed to run the woods in Oregon or Washington or someplace? You've seen those fake movies, haven't you? Bad, grainy, eight-millimeter shots of some naked guy with a lot of hair and beard tromping through the underbrush? They don't have sound but you can hear the grunts?"

"He didn't grunt his name for you?"

"He was very paranoid. No names." She clasped the empty tray to her chest with crossed arms. "He hung onto that book like this, wouldn't let anybody see the cover, only her picture. He didn't want questions, just answers: where was she. A week later he was back. It was sad. He'd lost the book. It figured. Charleen was dumb but she'd wised up a little here. He was childish. Naturally somebody ripped him off. He was lucky they left him his undershorts. He cried about the book, really cried, like a little kid. It was the only picture of Charleen he owned." She looked past Dave, frowned and nodded. "I've got to pick up an order. Look, I'm sorry I forgot before."

"One more second," Dave said. "Have you seen him lately? Big Foot?"

"No, it's been, what, two weeks? He was frantic. About the book. Thought he might have left it here. He hadn't." She tried to go inside. Dave stepped between her and the door.

"You never saw her with him? He didn't find her?"

"There are nine million people in this town. How could he find her? He was lost, himself." She tried to edge around him. "Look, I have to—"

"What about Spence Odum? Did you see her with him?"

"What's a Spence Odum?"

"A movie producer. You get film people in here."

"Did he tell you he was a producer?" she said. "They lie a lot, you know."

"A poster told me," Dave said. "In Charleen's apartment. Over her bed. He makes the kind of movies she might just luck into."

"I don't get told people's names much." A shout came from the dusky sunset room. "Sorry—I have to go," she said, and this time he let her.

Kids with soft-drink cans sat on the hood and trunk of the Triumph where he'd left it, halfway up the hill. Skate boarders curvetted past him. He didn't speak to the kids. When he stopped and took out keys, they got off the car.

The sky still held leftover daylight but when he tilted the Triumph up Horseshoe Canyon Trail the trees made it night. Big brown supermarket sacks crowded the passenger seat. He had to juggle with his knees to get a grip on them all. Slapped at by branches, he blundered through the dark to the cookhouse. He had to set the sacks down to unlock the door. Then it took him a while to find the light switch. The bulb that answered it was weak. He brought in the sacks and set them on a sink counter of cracked white tile that Amanda had already condemned.

She'd condemned the cabinets too—of greasy, varnished pine, none of the doors willing to stay shut. The stove and refrigerator, chipped white enamel, were probably good for another ten years, but she wanted him to have new ones. He wondered what color she would choose—copper, cinnabar, heliotrope? He emptied the sacks, stocked cupboards and refrigerator, where the bulb was out but the air was cold. He'd bought a plastic bag of ice cubes. He unwrapped a squat drink glass—he'd picked up six at the supermarket—dropped ice into it, and built a martini.

60

He left it to chill, crossed the uneven terra-cotta-tiled courtyard under beams from which vines hung in reaching tendrils, drooping big white trumpet flowers, to the third building, where fencing masks and foils rusted on knotty-pine walls. His stereo components sat on the dusty floor. He'd plugged them in and strung them together the day he hauled them up here from the rooms he'd shared with Doug above the gallery. Now he took the top album of the handiest stack and, without reading what it was, set the record on the turntable and started it going. The Mozart clarinet quintet. He turned up the volume, left the door open, and went back to the kitchen, the music trailing after him.

He'd forgotten to buy a can opener, but one hung off a divider between windows over the sink. Food from who knew what cans it had opened for how many years crusted the blade, but he overlooked that and cranked open a can of chili. He dumped the contents into one of his new supermarket aluminum saucepans and, while it heated, shredded lettuce with a dull, shiny supermarket knife onto a supermarket plate. He chopped up half an onion. There was no place to put the other half. He let it lie, shaved strings from a block of creamy Monterey jack cheese, then sat on the floor with his back against loose cabinet doors, drank the martini, listened to the music, and smelled the chili heating.

"You son of a bitch." Johnny Delgado stood in the doorway. He needed a shave. His clothes needed changing, had needed changing for some days. With a lot more gray in it than Dave remembered, his hair was shaggy and hung in his eyes. They glittered black in the bad light of the kitchen. He was unsteady on his feet. He hung onto the door frame and swayed. "You fucking vulture, perching in the trees, watching them tear me up, then coming down to feast off—feast off—the fucking carcass."

Dave got to his feet. "I can hardly find this place by daylight." The chili was bubbling. He set down his glass, turned the fire low, and gave the chili a stir with a shiny new perforated cooking spoon. "And sober. What kind of guidance system have you got?" He cranked open coffee, rinsed out the sections of the drip maker he'd also brought from the supermarket, and used a yellow plastic scoop to put coffee into it. He filled a pan with water and set it on a burner. "They didn't tear you up, Johnny. You tore yourself up."

"You took my job," Delgado said.

"I didn't take it," Dave said. He got the lettuce out of the bin in the bottom of the fridge and shredded another plateful and put the lettuce back. "You gave it back to Sequoia and they didn't know what to do with it, so they're handing out pieces of it. The piece I got is what I'm told I do best—a murder case with everything wrong with it."

"They never tried to get me." Delgado found a kitchen stepstool and sat on it. "They've got my phone number."

"They had one." Dave poured the chili over the beds of lettuce. "You'd left that place. No forwarding address." He strewed handfuls of cheese shavings on the chili, where it started to melt right away. "You also hadn't paid your bill in a while." He sprinkled on the chopped onion. "They told Sequoia that." He stripped cellophane off a glossy box that held cheap stainless-steel knives, forks, spoons. Each was in its own soft plastic sheath. He tore the sheaths off two forks, laid one fork on a plate, and held the plate out to Delgado. "It made a poor impression. So did the news that you were drunk all the time."

Delgado made a face at the plate. "I don't want that. What're you trying to do? Man, that takes balls. Steal somebody's job, then offer to feed him."

"I offer to feed you," Dave said, "because you're a friend, you're a guest in my house, I've got the food, and you need something in your stomach besides bourbon. Eat it, Johnny, or I'll put it in your hair." He pushed the plate at Delgado and Delgado grunted sourly and took it. He fumbled with the fork.

"This is a crazy place," he said.

"And that fact got it through escrow very fast." Dave stood at the counter and ate.

"I went over there." Delgado tilted his head. "Where the music's coming from. What is that place?"

"A man taught fencing there," Dave said. "Eat."

"If I throw up," Delgado said, "you deserve it." He filled his mouth. It opened. Chili dribbled down his chin. His eyes got big. "Jesus! Hot!"

"Cold chili never did much for me," Dave said.

Tilting the plate dangerously, Delgado got off the stool, kicked it aside, tore open the refrigerator door. Bottles of Dos Equis glittered on one of the wire shelves. He reached. "Beer. Yeah."

"Beer. No." Dave shut the door. He kicked the stool against the door and pushed Delgado down on it. The man gave off a stink of neglect. Dave had never seen him in any shirt but the white, short-sleeved kind with a tie. The tie had vanished and the shirt collar was greasy. "You eat now. Here's water if you have to wash it down." He dumped out the last of his martini, rinsed the glass, filled it, pushed it at Delgado, who was staring at the bottles of bourbon, scotch, and gin on the counter. Dave passed the glass in front of Delgado's eyes. "Drink."

Delgado waved a hand. He ducked his head over the plate and began shoveling down the chili. "Take it the fuck away. I hate the goddamn stuff. I'll eat. How do I get into situations like this?"

"Running around trying to find people to blame for the shambles you're in," Dave said. "Nobody else wants the blame any more than you do."

"Marie," Delgado said, with his mouth full. "She gets the blame." He laughed harshly, spraying chili, onions, cheese. "Why not? She got everything else—house, car, bank account. Let her have the blame." He pawed at the food stains on his shirt, his trousers. "Christ, I look like a goddamn wino." He got off the stool and set the plate on the counter. Shakily, so that it rattled. It was still half full. He looked into Dave's eyes. "Don't shove food down me, okay? Just leave me the hell alone?"

"I didn't come to your house." The water in the pan bubbled.

Dave poured it steaming into the waiting pot. "You came to my house, remember? Sit down. No, you don't have to eat any more. You can drink, now. Coffee. A whole lot of strong, black coffee."

Delgado started out the door. Dave dropped the empty pan clattering into the sink, took two long steps, and caught his arm. Delgado tried to jerk away. There was petulance in the gesture but not much strength. Under the soiled suitcoat, his arm felt wasted, an old man's, and he wasn't even forty. Dave turned him around and set him on the stool again. Delgado glared at him.

"And then what?" he said. "You push me into the shower, right? And I'm still not sober enough to drive? So you put me to bed to sleep it off? Am I on track? Sure, I am. And sometime in the night, you're in the bed with me. Yeah, oh, yeah." He nodded, mouth twisted in a sneer. He rubbed the stubble on his chin. A scrap of beef came away in his fingers, he flicked it off. "You know what you are and so do I, and that's tonight's scenario, isn't it?"

"You wrote it," Dave said. "You tell me." The Mozart turned itself off. The only sound was the drip of water through the coffee grounds and the whirr of crickets out in the sweaty canyon darkness. "You need a shower. You need clean clothes. I can lend you a sweatshirt and a pair of jeans. You are too drunk to drive. That doesn't matter. I can drive you home. Where are you living?"

"Crappy motel in Santa Monica," Delgado mumbled. "If they haven't locked me out."

Dave studied him. "You want to stay here, don't you? That's why you came. Not to chew me out for taking your job. To have a place to stay." He unwrapped a supermarket coffee mug, rinsed it under the tap, filled it with coffee. "You are broke. You're lonely." He held the mug out to Delgado, who was watching him with nothing in his bloodshot eyes. "You're also horny. And you're offering yourself in payment for anything I can do for you, only what mainly interests you is getting your rocks off."

Delgado made a sound and knocked the cup across the room.

Coffee splashed the cabinets and ran down. The cup was tough. It didn't break. Delgado lurched off the stool and stumbled out the door. On hands and knees, he vomited. The sounds he made were loud and miserable. Dave stood in the doorway trying to see in the poor light from the kitchen and from the building across the way whether a garden hose was coiled somewhere among the broken hibachis, splintered surfboards, and bent lawn furniture beneath the hanging vines. Delgado's stomach spasms eased off. He wiped a sleeve across his mouth.

"I warned you," he groaned. "You had to feed me. You just had to feed me."

"Come get some coffee," Dave said.

"You think I'd take anything from you now?" Delgado staggered to his feet. He spat. "Knowing what you think?"

"Is what I think any uglier than what you think? Come on. Forget it." He led Delgado back into the kitchen. He stood him at the sink. "Wash your face." Delgado splashed water with hands that hadn't seen any for a long time. Dave handed him a supermarket dishtowel. He picked up the fallen mug and poured coffee into it again. "Drink this. Take the shower. Sleep it off."

Silently, sullenly, Delgado did as he was told. Dave led him across to the room with the fencing masks. He lifted folded jeans and the promised sweatshirt out of a carton on the floor. He steered Delgado to the bathroom where grit crunched on the white tiles. He shut the door on Delgado, and while the shower splashed, he set up the steel frame, lowered onto it the box spring that had been leaning against the wall, the mattress. He lifted sheets and blankets from other cartons and made up the bed. The shower ceased.

"Don't try to shave tonight," Dave said. "Tomorrow."

He took a blanket for himself, left the building, closed the door behind him. He unlocked the big front building, threw the blanket inside, clicked light switches until somewhere outdoors around a corner a glow came from untrimmed brush. He went out again. Someplace he'd seen a garden hose. He went toward the light, shoes crackling dried oak leaves and eucalyptus seed pods. The smell of the eucalyptus was strong in the night heat. He found the hose. He prowled for a connection. He screwed the hose to it and turned the tap handle and got a lot of hard spray in his face. He dragged the hose around the house corner and reached the mess Delgado had made and, using his thumb to increase the force of the water, washed the vomit off the tiles into the littered earth under the shrubs.

"The midnight gardener," somebody said.

Dave turned. He knew the figure—slight, trim, the overgrown grounds-light behind him haloing gray hair. It was Doug, whom he'd lived with for three years and didn't live with anymore. "Right around to your left," he said, "is the turn-off. Turn it off for me?"

Doug stepped into shadow. He gave a yelp that said the leaky connection had doused him. The hose quit running and Dave dropped it. Doug came to him. He wore a safari jacket of crash linen with the cuffs turned back. He was brushing water off it. Dave asked, "What brings you here? Did Christian fling himself into a volcano?"

"I wanted to see if you were all right," Doug said.

The door of the building where the fencing masks hung opened. Delgado stood there in the fresh clothes. The light behind him shone off his wet hair. "Listen," he said, "I want to thank you. I feel a hell of a lot better."

"You sound better," Dave said. "There's a carton of medicine-chest stuff on the bathroom floor. Take some aspirin. It might ward off a headache in the morning."

"I hate taking your bed." Delgado saw Doug and jerked. "Oh, hell. Who's that?"

"Never mind me," Doug said. "Just carry on as if I hadn't come. Obviously, I shouldn't have."

"Ah, Christ," Delgado said. "Dave, I'm sorry."

"Nothing to be sorry for," Dave said. "Sleep well."

Delgado hesitated, then turned, slump-shouldered, went back inside, and shut the door.

"You can still surprise me," Doug said.

"You want some coffee?" Dave said.

9

Tapping woke him. He flinched at the brightness of the big empty room and thought extra windows might be a mistake. Groaning, he rolled onto his back on the creaky chaise he'd dragged in from the courtyard—webbing slack on a frame of aluminum tubing, the stuffing lumpy in the gaudy flower-print plastic pallet. He clutched the blanket around his nakedness and sat up. *Tap-tap-tap.* He squinted at the French doors. Where Amanda had made the circle on the dusty pane yesterday, she was smiling in at him. He lifted to her a hand that felt as if it belonged to someone else. It was early to smile, but he worked at it.

"You'll have to clear out," she called. "All sorts of physical types are coming with crowbars."

He pointed to the door, tottered into pants, and went barefoot to let her in. He raked fingers through his hair. His mouth tasted sour. He and Doug had drunk Dos Equis and munched tortilla chips until late—how late he didn't know. The talk had been guarded, mannerly, but he hoped Doug wouldn't keep coming back. What you used to have was only that. And what they used to have was flawed from the start. He'd lost Rod to cancer, Doug had lost Jean-Paul in a car smash. They'd tried to make the losses up to each other. Life didn't work that way. Love didn't work that way—if love worked any way. What did they coat those tortilla chips with? Rust-color dust. Garlic was what he tasted. He ran his tongue over his teeth and opened the door to Amanda. Her T-shirt read HIS TOO. She was in ninety-dollar jeans. She was ready for work.

"Someone's in your kitchen," she said. "A lovely, haggard Mediterranean type with long black eyelashes. He offered me coffee in a sultry voice. I was cagey. It could be doped. I could end up in a brothel in Turin."

"Or a motel in Santa Monica," Dave said, "which is worse. Go help him with the bacon and eggs. If he makes any false moves, holler, and I'll come running. Soapy and stark naked but running."

"Promises," she said, and went to the cookhouse.

Dave hobbled and hopped to the fencing studio. Getting there barefoot was painful. A countertenor was having to do with Monteverdi when he switched on the radio. He rifled cartons for clothes and went into the bathroom. When he came out, showered and shaved, the music was piano and violin, something twentieth-century. Delgado and Amanda sat on the side of the bed and ate from plates on their knees. Mugs of coffee steamed at their feet. Delgado started to get up but Dave went to the cookhouse, got his own plate from the oven where it was keeping warm, poured himself a mug of coffee, and went back with them. He sat on the other side of the bed, drank some coffee to wash out the mint taste of the tooth powder, and swallowed some eggs.

"The car is full of catalogues for you to look at," Amanda said. "Sample books. Fabrics. Carpet. Furniture. I hope you haven't got a big day's work planned."

"I can work for him," Delgado said. He looked over his shoulder at Dave. "Who should I talk to?"

"Spence Odum. Maybe he knows where Charleen Sims is. Only

you have to find him first. I've checked the directories. He doesn't have a business address. He doesn't even have a home address. He makes skinflicks."

"I'll find him for you," Delgado said. "What do you want with Charleen what's-her-name?"

"I think it's possible she witnessed a murder."

Delgado was making Dave feel guilty about having checked the liquor bottles in the kitchen. He knew drunks. Delgado must have awakened feeling rotten. The remedy for that was to jolt down alcohol as soon as possible. To stop the shaking, the panic. The gin bottle was the only one Dave had opened himself. It didn't seem any emptier than when he'd made his martini. The seals on the Jack Daniels and the Glenlivet were intact. He said, "You don't have to do it."

"I'd like to," Delgado said. "Maybe if I do it right, you'll put in a word for me at Sequoia."

"You'll do it right," Dave said. "Maybe she didn't call herself Sims. Maybe it was Dawson. For what my advice is worth—I doubt that Odum belongs to any guilds. I doubt that he belongs to the Motion Picture Academy."

"I don't doubt that he drives a car," Delgado said.

"Two hundred a day and expenses," Dave said.

"No way." Delgado gulped the last of his coffee. "Twenty bucks for gas and lunch. And I wouldn't take that if I wasn't broke." He set the mug on the plate and stood. "I'll wash the dishes and get going."

"You're locked out of your motel," Dave reminded him.

"That's not your problem." Delgado took Amanda's mug and plate and started for the door. "Maybe I tried to make it your problem last night, but it's not."

"Don't worry about the dishes," Dave said. "You cooked the breakfast. My wallet's in the front building on the floor by the thing I slept on. Better take fifty. It gets expensive out there. You don't want to run short."

"Let me have those." Amanda took the plates out of Delgado's hands and went out into the leaf-speckled sunlight with them. Halfway across the courtyard she called back, "And good luck." She went into the cookhouse and water began splashing there.

Dave sat and finished his breakfast. He heard the door of the front building close and the crunch of Delgado's steps rounding the house and fading toward his car. But there was no noise of the car starting. Swallowing the last of his eggs, he got to his feet. He left the plate with Amanda at the sink and carried his coffee out to the front. Delgado leaned in under the raised hood of an old Pontiac with a smashed-out taillight. A pocketknife was in his hand. He was trying to make it serve as a screwdriver to fasten some wires. He saw Dave and straightened up, banging his head. He rubbed his head, wincing. But it didn't hide the guilt in his eyes.

"Relax," Dave said. "You fixed it so you could stamp off mad at me, or go off rejected and dejected, or however the scene played itself, and you wouldn't be able to get your car started. You'd have to stay. I've had it done to me before."

Delgado stared, making up his mind about whether or not to get sore. He bent back under the hood and worked with the wires again. "There's something you don't know about people," he said. "There has to be. It stands to reason." He grunted with the effort of what he was doing. "There." He got out from under the hood and slammed it shut. He folded up the jackknife and dropped it into the pocket of the jeans Dave had lent him.

Dave said, "When people run out of probable things to do, they do improbable things. That's all. Nothing so wonderful about that."

Delgado opened the door on the driver's side and got into the car. The door squeaked. Cotton wadding stuck out of a worn place in the seat. He started the engine and shut the door. "Only you don't get surprised," he said.

"Once or twice," Dave said. "It's dangerous. I don't like it. But

I know it's going to happen again. The odds are like that. I haven't met everybody in the world, yet. It only feels that way."

Delgado had made a bundle of his dirty clothes. It lay on the seat beside him. He must have put it there when he got up. He said, "I know what you mean."

"The trick is to remember that they only seem the same," Dave said. "They're not the same. And one of them is waiting to surprise the hell out of me."

"I hope it isn't me," Delgado said.

Dave slapped the window ledge and stepped back. "Good luck," he said. "Call me when you locate Spence Odum. Wait, I didn't give you my number."

Delgado grinned. "I swiped a card out of your wallet." He backed the car. Dust huffed from under the worn tires. The old engine rattled a lot at the effort it had to make getting up the rutted drive to the trail. Delgado raised a hand and let the Pontiac roll down the potholed blacktop. It backfired a couple of times. Dave didn't let himself think about how many drinks fifty dollars would buy. He went back to the cookhouse and helped Amanda with the dishes.

After that they sat cross-legged on the floor in the big room and looked at shiny pictures of objects to sit on and to eat off of, they ran their hands on carpet samples, fingered swatches of fabric meant to cover chairs and hang at windows. A gnarled man with one arm and two big, speechless sons arrived in a ranchero wagon and tramped around scowling at the work to be done. A lot of adding up took place on the backs of envelopes—brick, lumber, masonry, manhours, sheet metal, wiring, tile. A rattly pickup truck with board sides jolted into the yard and an old Japanese couple hauled gardening tools out of it. A chain saw began to snarl. When the brown old woman in man's hat and shoes shut it off for a minute, Dave heard the telephone. It was in the fencing room. He ran for it.

"This is Midnight," the voice at the other end said.

"Noon," Dave said. He glanced at his watch. "Ten minutes to one, as a matter of fact."

"No, man—Richie Midnight." Restaurant noises were behind the voice. "Back in Wisconsin it's still Mittelnacht, but how do you expect a deejay to pronounce that? How do you expect to put that on an album cover?"

"There's Engelbert Humperdinck," Dave said. "But let it pass. You found Charleen, right? What did she do, come in to dance again?"

"She didn't come in. I didn't find her. But I sure as hell went looking for her. She's dead, man. She's got to be. Disappeared when Dawson got killed, that joker she was with? Nobody's seen her. I mean, she was visible, audible, right? Everybody on the Strip knew her. Only way somebody like that could disappear is they're dead."

"Your friend Priss estimates LA at nine million souls," Dave said. "It's more likely she's just mislaid."

"That's not in very good taste," Mittelnacht said.

"Don't be so eager to cry," Dave said. "I don't know how much death you've seen, but it's not romantic."

"I was in Nam," Mittelnacht said.

"Did they teach you how to break necks?" Dave asked.

"They taught me how to mainline horse. And not to bitch at all the lousy pianos they gave me to play."

"None of this is what you called about," Dave said. "What did you call about?"

"There's this jock I ran into. He's around the Strip a lot. I mean, I don't know him. I know him. You know what I mean? He's not a close friend, just a dude. An actor. Only there's just one reason he ever gets cast. He's got this tremendous organ of procreation, right? And—"

"So he worked for Spence Odum," Dave said.

"You got it. And he knows where Odum's shooting."

"Tell me," Dave said.

10

The building with the number Mittelnacht had given him faced the Strip and looked all wrong. The facade was colonial—white pillars, green shutters. A sign claimed real estate was sold behind the green door with the shiny brass knocker. Dave waited for a break in traffic, then skidded the Triumph around a corner where the side street dropped sharply. There was an alley. He nipped into it. Spaces for cars backed on the rear walls of shops, trash barrels, broken crates. The barred, employees-only doors were mostly unnumbered. But a number matching that on the real-estate office was lettered in runny white paint on a plywood door where a tall girl in noticeable makeup and a costume of pink, red, and orange skirts, scarves, and sashes smoked a cigarette under a yellow turban with a cerise plume. He pulled the Triumph in beside a white van without lettering that somehow didn't look like anybody's vacation vehicle—it looked like business, anonymous business. The girl wore big fake-gold hoop earrings and had a husky voice. She looked Dave up and down hungrily and said with a regretful smile:

"Sorry. Nobody gets in."

The door opened. A college-age boy in glasses and with a prominent Adam's apple said, "Okay, he wants you."

"Excuse me," the tall girl said, "it's the big moment in the torture chamber." She dropped the cigarette, stepped on it with a gold sandal that showed toenails glued with glitter, and went inside. Dave went inside after her.

Before the door fell shut, daylight showed him washrooms littered with wigs, greasepaint tubes, boxes of tan powder, crumpled tissues stained with lipstick. NO SMOKING, a sign said. Then the door closed and the only light was out in a big brick room where it struck hard at a naked teenage girl struggling inside a gilt-and-crimson papier-mâché mummy case that stood upright. Shiny manacles held the girl's ankles and wrists, chains looping from them to cleats inside the case. The case had a split lid, the curved halves open. The tall girl stood to one side of the coffin, another dressed like her to the other side. Silhouetted against the light, a pair of men flanked a camera on a tripod. The only sound was the whir of the camera motor. The girl screamed silently and writhed without conviction in the very loose chains, while the gaudy attendants slowly closed the lethal halves of the door. Thirty percent shut. Eighty percent.

"Freeze it there." The man who spoke had golliwog hair. He was big, barrel-shaped, soft. He moved out into the dazzling light— black suit, black cape, pasted-on mandarin moustache. He undid the manacles. The naked girl stepped out of the mummy case. Her hair was tawny, her skin tawny, flawless over a layer of puppy fat. She went away into the shadows. The gaudily rigged girls stood deathly still. The fuzzy-haired man returned to the camera. "All right." He ducked his head, did something to his face. "One second for makeup. Now! Camera? Action!" The motor whirred again. The gaudy girls went back to shutting the mummy case.

At the last moment, cape flying, a slouch hat hiding his mad hair, the man rushed into the light. He flung himself against the doors, jamming them shut. He swung to face the camera. He'd put on a domino mask. He raised a fist at the camera, threw back his head and laughed in demented triumph. He'd fitted himself with joke-store Dracula teeth. He held the pose. He held the pose. Sweat trickled from under the mask. He held the pose. He broke the pose.

"Zoom, you asshole!" he shouted. "Zoom—remember?"

"Oh, shit, I'm sorry, Spence," the cameraman said.

Spence looked at the ceiling. "Herman, where are you when I need you?" He sighed, wiped his face. "Okay. Get it right this time." He turned back to the mummy case, leaned his hands against it, whirled, repeated the fist-shaking, the crazy laugh. He held the pose. The cameraman worked something on the camera. Spence held the pose. He broke it.

"Cut." He untied the cape and let it fall, made a face and took out the teeth. "That gets it." He dropped the teeth into a pocket. "Strike the mummy case."

"Don't you want the blood running out of it?" The boy with the Adam's apple came into the light holding a floppy script, blue covers, big brass brads. "That's the next shot you wrote down here."

"Not while I've got actors sitting around getting paid," Spence said.

Derisive laughter came from the dark.

"We haven't got ketchup right now, anyway," Spence said. "I'll smuggle a couple bottles out of Fatburger after supper."

"Cheap, cheap!" voices chanted from the dark.

Spence took off the domino. "Move it out," he said. "And let's have some worklights for a minute, okay?"

Someone warm, smooth, and naked brushed past Dave. Light switches clicked. The big brick room had walls of assorted colors. Against a red section, a dummy slouched in an antique barber chair. Above a wing collar, the dummy's plaster throat was cut. The head lolled back. Memory said something to Dave about a demon barber of Fleet Street. Manacles and chains draped a blue section of wall above a wood-frame torture device with ropes and a big wheel—a rack? A brazier with fake glowing goals had fake branding irons sticking out of it.

The switcher-on of lights brushed past Dave again. He was perhaps twenty, blond, smoothly muscled as a Roman marble. He wore his economical young flesh as unerotically as clothes. He went and sat on a butt-sprung daybed with a tattered spread of black velvet sewed with sequins. The girl from the mummy case sat there too, smoking a cigarette, legs crossed. The boy picked up a Coke can from the cement floor and drank from it. The boy with the Adam's apple, and another boy even younger and wearing earphones with the cord dangling, got the mummy case onto a two-wheeled dolly to cart it out of the way. Spence called to them:

"Easy. Don't bang it around. I want to use it in my next billion-dollar box-office smash. As a bathtub full of champagne."

"Ginger ale," one of the tall girls said.

"How about a sports car?" the naked boy said. "Paint on lights and a grill. Tack on some wheels. Let it roll off a cliff and catch fire. Just like TV. Sensational."

"Varoom!" Spence said, studying a script. He flapped over pages. "Okay, where's Inspector Hardcock of the CID?"

A middle-aged man said "Hah!" and came out of a corner where a brass bed glistened against purple-flocked wallpaper. He tucked his script under his arm, put a deerstalker cap on his bald head, set a meerschaum pipe in his teeth. He wore a moustache and a tweed suit, and he chuckled.

"This is fascinating," he said. "Why don't you film it in order?"

"I'll be lucky," Spence said, "if I can get it in order when I edit it. Where's the gun? I didn't give you the gun, did I?" He went past the couch where the naked youngsters sat and rummaged in a curve-topped trunk that had been gold-leafed and stuck all over with glass jewels. He came up with a tin pistol and tossed it to the middle-aged man. He went to a tall flat, painted to match the brick wall. The flat had a door in it. "You come in here. Bursting in, you know? Only be careful. It's only lath and cardboard." He squinted at a pair of heavy-headed lights on standards that flanked the door. He looked around. "Randy? Do me a favor, baby? Get these out of here. Out the back. I'm tired of moving them for every shot."

The girl who had let Dave in went and picked up the lamps. She was strong. She brought them past Dave. They creaked and squeaked and nodded. The girl widened her mascaraed eyes at him. She muttered, "How the fuck did you get in? You're going to be in trouble."

"It should happen to everybody once," Dave said, and pushed open the door for her. The sun was bright and hot out there. Clumsy in the skirts and scarves, she wrestled the lights outside. They clanked and clashed. Bright metal tags were riveted to them. The tags read SUPERSTAR RENTALS. Dave let the door fall shut. Spence was lecturing the middle-aged man in the deerstalker cap.

"You've discovered Doctor Dreadful's House of Horrors at last. You've been running all over Soho in the fog looking for it. You stare all around. You're appalled, right? We'll keep cutting in shots of the mummy case, the torture instruments, the dead dummy, all of it. So take your time. Then there they are—the kids you've been trying to protect. You gape at them. Really shocked, okay? You've come too late, all right?" He turned. "Junie? Harold?"

"Oh, shit, here it comes." Harold set down his Coke on the floor and pushed his beauty up off the couch. He looked abused and resentful. "This is where I have to carry her, isn't it?"

"That's rude." The girl called Junie uncrossed her legs, bent, and stubbed out her cigarette on the cement. "You know how I diet and diet." She got up, shaking back her hair.

Spence said, "You come in from over there by the washrooms, holding her in your arms. You walk into camera range right past here, got it? You stop where the tape is on the floor. Only don't look down for it, this time, okay? Feel it with your toes. You're stunned. No expression. That ought to be easy. Just stare at the Inspector. Junie, you've passed out from pain, remember? So let your head hang back, way back. Be dead weight in his arms, right?"

"Aw, Spence." The naked boy trudged back to Dave.

"It'll be over before you know it," Spence said.

"I hope you've got a truss in that trunk," Harold said.

"That would look fetching in the sex scenes," Spence said. "Bend your knees when you lift her. You'll be fine."

Junie grinned. "Be thankful he never makes retakes."

"Never use that word in my presence," Spence said.

"Do I have to pick her up now?" Harold said.

"Once for practice," Spence said. "You don't have to carry her till Hardcock comes in and starts looking around."

"Yeah, looking around *slowly,*" Harold said. He blew air out through his nose. Disgustedly he got into a half crouch and held out his arms. "Come on, Pudgy."

But Junie saw Dave. "There's a strange man here."

"What?" Spence saw Dave too. He came over. "This is a closed set," he said. "What do you want?"

"To know where Charleen Sims is." Dave took out his wallet and showed Spence his license. "She told people she had a job in films. You're Spence Odum, right? She's got a poster from one of your productions on a wall over her bed. In an apartment she left hurriedly ten days ago and hasn't come back to. I don't suppose your posters get around much."

"We're very big in Possum Stew, Arkansas," Spence Odum said, "and Gopher Hole, Nebraska. But not in Ninevah and Tyre." He gave his wristwatch a pained look. "Listen, I'm on a very tight budget. I can't hang around talking. Who?"

"Charleen Sims," Dave said, "or maybe Charleen Dawson."

"Never heard of her," Spence Odum said.

"I'm suffocating back here." The middle-aged man opened the painted cardboard door in the painted cardboard flat. "If I have to turn this knob, I've got to use my right hand. The gun will have to be in my left hand."

"We'll run through it," Odum called without turning.

"Blond, small, slender," Dave said. "Possibly as old as sixteen but she looks twelve."

Odum clowned shock, eyes wide, fingers to mouth. "But—but," he stammered, "that's—why, that's—degenerate!" He held an open hand out to the naked young people who laughed. "Do I look like that sort of man?" He turned to the big brick room, holding out his arms. The cameraman was grinning. So were the boys stowing the mummy case in a corner. "Do you see anything decadent about this operation, anything depraved?" He turned back to Dave, taking off the slouch hat, clutching it to his breast. "I hope you won't spread that opinion around. It could ruin my future with Walt Disney Productions."

Junie giggled. Harold and the crew guffawed.

"It's Charleen's future that worries me," Dave said. "She's mixed up in murder. She may even have been murdered herself. Now, do you know anything about her?"

The laughter stopped. Odum looked sober. "No. I don't. I never met her, never heard of her. I don't know where she got the poster. Everybody rips everything off these days. You know that. I wouldn't use her. Too young. Truth." He turned away, turned back. "Why would somebody murder her?"

"Because she saw Gerald Dawson murdered," Dave said.

Odum moistened his lips. "Superstar Rentals?"

"The place you get your stuff from," Dave said.

"I don't know the girl," Odum said. "Believe me." He read his watch again. "Look, will you get out, now, please?"

"I'll be back," Dave said and left.

Blinded by sunlight, he was inside the Triumph before he noticed that Randy was in it ahead of him, in her hoop earrings and beaded false lashes. She gave off a powerful incense smell. "You want to buy me a drink?" she said in her husky voice. "Or do you want me to buy you a drink? Women's lib and all that. We could have dinner. It's not too early."

Dave still couldn't see so he reached out and laid fingers on her face. Under the heavy makeup was beard stubble. He laughed and turned the key in the ignition. The Triumph started with a splutter of loud little valves. He backed out of the shadow of the white van. "I have to see somebody at the marina," he said. "Do you like to eat at the marina?"

"I like to sit and drink mai tais at the Warehouse and watch the little boats sink in the west."

"It's those tiny parasols they attach to the mai tais." The Triumph raced down the alley and into the street. "Poor butterfly and all that, right?"

" 'Neath the blossoms waiting," Randy sighed.

The decor at the Warehouse was barrels and cargo nets. On the wooden decks big pots of flowers perched on tarry pier stakes. It was three. Most of the lunch tables stood empty. The tourists had gone away with their neck-strap Minoltas full of out-of-focus blue water and white boats. The boats tilting around the long, narrow bay had sails striped red and orange. The moored boats sported blue canvas covers. None of these was Fullbright's. Fullbright's was over yonder. He'd visit it next.

"No," Randy Van said, "Spence doesn't want to be fooled. He knows I'm a TV. Does he ever! If he could figure out how, TV's are all he'd use. But for obvious reasons, at least one girl has always got to be real." He twisted the dinky bamboo-and-tissue-paper parasol off his drink in fingers with scarlet nails. He'd abandoned the turban and most of the scarves in the Triumph out on the lot by the big wooden tanks of koi fish. He smiled at Dave. "Boo-hoo," he said. "Reality is always messing up my life."

"It can't be a career," Dave said. "He doesn't make any money. He couldn't pay union scale."

"Be serious." Randy sipped at the big drink that looked like laboratory blood. "He pays eighty a day, but even if he paid scale, he shoots in two days. Then he lays off for months. My career is running a double-needle sewing machine in a loft full of lady Mexican illegals. They think they're a persecuted minority. Hah!"

"He says he never used a skinny little tyke called Charleen. Blond? Hardly out of grammar school. Did he?"

"Never." Randy shook his head. It loosened his wig that was shiny black Medusa curls. He set it tight with both hands. "I've worked in every flick he's made, so I know. If he wanted to, he couldn't. The Iowa hicks that line up Saturday nights on main street would be outraged. Down Alabama way, they'd burn out the theater." Randy sipped his mai tai. A lot of lipstick had accumulated on the rim of the glass. "I mean, he wants me, but he sighs and hires big tits and lots of corn-fed ass. Like Junie."

"She looks like a college girl," Dave said.

"Pepperdine." Randy nodded. "She does it for laughs." He cocked an eyebrow. "You didn't think it was hard-core, did you? Oh, no. She and Harold will roll around naked on that brass bed and kiss and moan a lot, but that's all. The rednecks would burst a blood vessel if anything really happened. That's what skinflick means—what you see ain't what you think, but it makes you think it is."

"And he shoots them in two days?" Dave asked.

"On a lavish ten thousand bucks. Can I have a cigarette?" Dave pushed his pack across the shiny planks of the tabletop. He lighted cigarettes for both of them. "Thanks," Randy said. "Most of the budget goes on lights, equipment, studio rent. Music? He sneaks tape recorders into jazz clubs. Crew? College film students who want the experience and beg for the chance. Pay? What's pay?"

"Cameraman too?" Dave said.

"Now," Randy said. "Before, it was always Herman."

"Before what? Odum misses him. Where is he?"

"Dead. Herman Ludwig. Some kind of refugee from behind the Iron Curtain." Randy winced. "That expression always makes my teeth hurt. He was supposed to have been famous in Europe. Once upon a time." Randy gazed out at the curvetting boats, the gleaming water. He blew away smoke. "He was shot. On the parking lot in back of the studio. Late at night. Those two days usually stretch their full twenty-four hours. Spence was setting up. Herman went out to bring back coffee. And somebody blew his head off with a shotgun."

"Who?" Dave said. "When?"

"Nobody knows who. They just shot him and drove off. We didn't hear it. The place is soundproof. The sheriff found out later that neighbors heard it but nobody phoned in. I got sent out to find him when he didn't come back. I stumbled across him. Dear God." Unsteadily Randy gulped down all that remained of his mai tai. "Talk about your hair turning white in one night!"

"When?" Dave said again.

"Oh—what? Ten days ago? Spence really misses him."

Lieutenant Ken Barker of the LAPD said, "The Strip's not even city, you know that. It's county. You have to see the sheriff." He sat behind a green steel desk strewn with file folders, report forms, photographs. It was in a room partitioned off by glass and green steel from a wide glass-and-green-steel room where telephones jangled, typewriters rattled, men laughed, coughed, grumbled. Barker's nose was broken. His shoulders strained the seams of his shirt. His collar was open, tie dragged down, cuffs turned back. He was sweating. He drank from a waxed-paper cup printed with orange swirls. Shaved ice rattled in the cup. He set it down. "Christ, is this weather ever going to let up?"

"It's too much of a coincidence," Dave said.

"Two murders a night? It's damn near normal. You tell me how they could be more different—a broken neck in Hillcrest, a shotgun blast away out west in a parking lot."

"There's a connection," Dave said. "Spence Odum rents his lights and cameras and recorders from the company Dawson was a partner in."

"Don't a lot of people?" Barker said. "How many outfits like that are there? From what you tell me about Odum's operation, they sure as hell couldn't keep solvent if he was their only customer."

"He was their only customer who had a cameraman murdered the same night as Dawson," Dave said. "And that's not all. Dawson was sleeping with a teenage hooker called Charleen something, who told people on the Strip she was about to get into the movies, and who had a poster from a Spence Odum picture on her wall, and who disappeared the same night as Dawson and Ludwig died."

"They go off," Barker said. "The prowl cars see them every night, like matches in the dark. And then they don't see them anymore. Some middle-aged account executive with holes in his superego takes them on a expense-account jet ride to Vegas, some john, right? And strands them there. So they sit in some casino with a dead drink in one hand and a silver dollar in the other till the next john offers them twenty bucks, bed, and breakfast—and the next, and the next."

"Till they meet some crazy," Dave said, "who carves them up and puts them in a plastic bag with your name and address on it. I thought of that."

Barker's eyes were gunmetal color, about the same gray as his hair. They regarded Dave for a few seconds. "You are a terrible man," he said. "Did you know that?"

"You've got one now," Dave said.

Barker stood up, chair backing to deepen a dent in file cabinets behind him. "Skinny little blond. We've had her for a week. No ID."

The body didn't make much of a rise in the sheet that covered it. It didn't take up much room on the long steel slab the attendant in the green smock pulled on silent rollers out of a wall. Barker laid the sheet back. She had hardly any breasts at all. She was greenish pale except for the slash down her front made by the medical examiner and the cut where her scalp had been laid back and then replaced. The hair was the color of sun-bleached southwest hillside grass—between yellow and white. There were bruises on her throat, scratches.

"Strangled," Dave said.

Barker opened a file folder. "Right. Also skull fracture. Also raped. And"—he pulled the sheet all the way down—"she once had polio. One leg shorter than the other." Dave looked at it. It was sticklike, the knee a pitiful outsize knob. He took the edge of the sheet and covered the girl up again.

"I don't think it's her," he said. "Nobody mentioned any limp. One of my witnesses said she danced well. This one may have danced—I hope so—but it can't have been well." He called thanks to the attendant.

In the elevator, Barker said, "Did Odum tell you he hired your girl—Charleen?"

"He only got nervous," Dave said, "and pressed for time."

They got off the elevator. "Did you ask him about Ludwig?"

"I didn't know about Ludwig then," Dave said.

"You don't know about him now." Back at his desk, Barker emptied a heavy, sharp-cornered glass ashtray into a metal wastebasket. "He was in this country illegally. Ludwig wasn't even his name. He was scared to use it. He was scared to surface enough even to work where he might be noticed—Columbia, Paramount."

"He had a big reputation in Europe," Dave said.

"Oh, so you do know," Barker said.

"I know that," Dave said. "What else is there?"

"The Hungarian party had it in for him. His story was they were chasing him all over the world to kill him." The telephone on Barker's desk rang. He lifted the receiver, listened a minute, grunted "Thanks," and hung up. He looked at Dave. "And they found him. And they killed him, didn't they?"

"Why was he illegal? A prominent artist—they don't have trouble defecting. 'I lift my lamp beside the—' "

"It would make headlines. The baddies would get him."

"Sounds like paranoia to me," Dave said.

"The kind that gets you killed," Barker said.

"Maybe," Dave said. "It's neat but neatness isn't everything." He stood up. "So who do I see at the sheriff's department? You know all about it. So you looked into it. So you thought the way I think—that there might be some connection. Who do I talk to over there?"

"Salazar," Barker said. "But it's the way I told you. Ask Ludwig's widow if you want confirmation. Salazar will give you her address."

Dave picked up the receiver of Barker's phone. "How do I get an outside line?" he said.

The apartment was old tan brick, down a side street from Melrose in Hollywood. The windows were small. Cracked plaster Egyptian pillars flanked the door to a dark hallway that went straight to the back. At one side of the hallway, stairs went up. They were about to be boxed in by walls and a door. New fire regulations. The framework of two-by-fours was already in. The smell of fresh-sawn pine was pleasant, nearly covering the sad, sour smell of too many decades of living that seeped through the desperately fresh paper on the walls, the hopelessly fresh carpeting he walked on.

Number six was the last door in the downstairs hallway. After he pressed the buzzer he looked out the rear window. A pair of cats lay curled asleep in the sun on the green tin lid of a big trash module by a chain-link fence. Marigolds struggled in a strip of parched earth against the fence. He saw the stucco corner of a garage. A lock clicked inside the door. The varnish on the door was laid over fifty years of earlier varnish and was nearly black. The door opened four inches. The face that peered at him was bone white, almost fleshless, with fierce patches of rouge. Black lines had been drawn around eyes large, dark, but more annoyed than frightened.

"What do you want?" She had a thick accent and her voice was a gasp. "Who are you?"

"My name is Brandstetter." He held open his wallet so she could read the license. "I'm an insurance investigator."

"My husband did not have." She tried to close the door. He put his foot in it. "Please. I have no time."

"Another man was murdered on the same night as your husband," Dave told her. "It's about his death I want to talk to you. I think the two might be connected. Someone innocent is going to suffer if I can't clear the matter up."

Her laugh was harsh and turned into a hacking cough. "Someone innocent is going to suffer? That will be a novelty in this world." Her eyes went angry, her voice scornful. "The innocent are always the ones who suffer. What kind of man are you, not to know that?"

"I told you," Dave said. "The kind that wants to prevent it. If I can. You want to help me or not?"

She shut the door. A chain rattled. She opened the door. The rest of her was as wasted as her face. She clutched an armload of clothes to the flat bosom of a faded shirt. A green dish towel was tied over her hair. From what he could see of it, the hair was sparse. It started far back on her brow. She wore jeans that hung off skeletal hips. The jeans weren't roomy—she'd shrunk away inside them. He thought she was very sick and that she had once been very beautiful. She went and laid the armload of clothes in a big scuffed leather suitcase that lay open on a Danish couch with scratched woodwork and threadbare plaid cushions. A small suitcase lay on a chair. There was a brand-new, shiny red metal footlocker.

"Who was this other fortunate man?" she asked.

"Gerald Dawson. His business was renting film equipment. The camera your husband used. For Spence Odum."

"I do not know him." She lit a cigarette, the old-fashioned kind, short and thick, no tip. The first intake of smoke started her coughing. It wracked her, bent her over. It sounded like ripping canvas. The cigarette hanging in her garishly lipsticked mouth, she clung to the back of a chair till the coughs stopped shaking her. She whispered, "He never mentioned the name. Was he Hungarian? It sounds like not a Hungarian name. Dawson?"

"He was an American who went to church a lot."

Her wry smile showed teeth of surprising whiteness and evenness. He'd thought she was fifty. The teeth said thirty. "They would not be friends," she said. "My husband was an artist, an intellectual. He regarded religion as superstition." The cigarette bobbed as she spoke. Smoke from it trickled up into an eye. She squinted that eye. "He distrusted systems of thought. He felt they cramped the mind and made fools of people." She went into a farther room and came back with another armload of clothes. "He said religion only caused hatred and bloodshed. He was an intelligent man and a gifted one. You must not think he filmed only sex pictures for vermin like this Spence Odum."

"I don't," Dave said. "Why did he do it here?"

She knelt to lay the clothes in the footlocker. She looked up at Dave. "He had made enemies in Hungary. He would not keep quiet about the horrors of the regime. When they tried and jailed a friend who was a writer, he spoke out. If he had not fled, they would have killed him."

"But he never made any speeches in the West," Dave said. "He didn't come out as a dissident. He didn't lay charges about this writer."

"For my sake," she said. "For the sake of relatives left behind in Hungary."

"So he was out of the way and was no harm to them," Dave said. "Why would they come here and kill him?"

She shrugged and stood. Sick as she looked, she moved like a girl, a girl trained in grace. Maybe she'd been an actress. "He would not tell me what lay behind his fear. He wanted me to know nothing in case I should be caught and tortured."

"Did you ever think perhaps he imagined it?"

"He did not imagine his own death," she said. "That was quite a reality, was it not?"

"Yes, but the killer hasn't been caught," Dave said. "Maybe it wasn't someone from Hungary. Maybe instead it had to do with Gerald Dawson's murder."

"No." She shook her head. "They were following him. Always. He saw them in Portugal, and the same ones again in Brazil, and the same ones again in Canada."

"He saw them," Dave said. "Did you see them?"

"No, I did not, but that means nothing." She looked hard at Dave. "He was not mad. How can you think that when this has happened?"

"What about here?" Dave said. "Did he tell you he'd seen them here?"

"No. He told me we had escaped them at last." Bitterly she twisted out her cigarette in an ashtray on a cheap teak-veneer end table. A lamp whose tweedy white shade years and cigarette smoke had yellowed stood on the table. So did a five-by-seven photograph in a dime-store frame. She picked up the photograph and gazed at it. "And then, in a dark parking lot, seven thousand miles from Budapest, they killed him." With a sleeve of the old blouse she wiped the glass on the photograph and laid it on the folded clothes in the footlocker. She stood looking down at it, motionless. "And now, I can go home." She turned Dave the wry smile again. "I never said it to him, of course—but I was dying to go home." A bleak laugh rustled in her throat. "Now I am going home to die. Isn't it funny?"

Dave didn't answer. He had stepped over to the footlocker. He was looking down at the photograph. It was black-and-white. Against a background of river and bridge, a man and woman stood close. The woman was lovely. A breeze blew the picture hat she wore, fluttered the ribbons. She hung onto the hat and smiled at the camera. Her arm was around the waist of a big, grinning man, barrel-shaped, soft-looking. Frizzy fair hair stood out all over his head.

12

The sun bulged out as it got to ocean level. It was bloated and smoky red. He stood at the end of the long, white-painted pier and watched it go down. Sailing craft, power craft passed, headed for moorings. Sounds drifted to him from the boats, high children's voices, a man's laugh, someone having poor luck with a guitar. A crowd of heavy-bodied pelicans splashed down awkwardly into the red water. The wings of circling gulls were like porcelain, the red light shining through them. Nearby, ice cubes rattled in a martini pitcher. The tang of charcoal smoke reached him. He wanted a drink. He wanted to eat. He was tired. But when he'd been here earlier with Randy Van, the flame-color 260Z hadn't stood in the fenced and guarded parking lot belonging to this pier. Now the car was there. So he had to do this.

He clambered aboard a shiny white fiberglass cabin cruiser. It wasn't the biggest or showiest craft along here but it was big and showy enough, forty-five, fifty feet. The rear deck he stepped onto was glowing teak planks. Brass rails gleamed. He opened a pair of glossy hatch doors and a teak companionway took him down into a teak cabin with brass lanterns, buttoned cowhide couches, thick carpet. A stereo played softly. This, the car, the fact the cabin wasn't locked, all said he should be here. But he could be in a restaurant. That would be nice. Dave opened a door at the far end of the cabin. Beds were in the next cabin—not bunks, beds. He heard the splash of a shower.

Above the beds were cabinets. He stepped up on a bed and looked into the cabinets. Sheets, blankets, a life jacket, no carton. He stepped up on the other bed and the carton wasn't in those cabinets either. He got down and knelt and opened storage drawers under the beds. Clothes. Boat gear. He stood up, and one of the cabinet doors had swung open, and he rapped his skull on it. From beyond the door to the head, a male voice called, over the noise of the shower:

"Help yourself to a drink, baby. Fix me a G and T, will you? I'll be out in a minute."

Dave went into the forward cabin again and searched drawers under the cowhide couches. Cameras. Skin-diving stuff. No carton. He shut the drawers, looked around him, went behind a small bar. The carton stood on the floor. He picked it up, set it on the bar, put on his reading glasses. The flap corners of the carton had been tucked under each other to keep it closed. He tugged them up. Raw film was supposed to be in the box. It wasn't. A ledger lay there. He lifted it out and opened it. The entries went back more than five years. The handwriting was always the same though the pens used were different. The bookkeeping wasn't fancy—just amounts paid and by whom, never for what. The customer's names didn't tell him much—except Spence Odum's. The light wasn't good coming in through brass-bound portholes off the water. The music whispered. Small waves lisped against the hull. The boat very gently rocked. He laid the ledger on the bar.

Next in the box lay manila folders. In alphabetical order by customer name, the same names as those in the ledger. The folders held copies of invoices. Written by hand, not typed, by the same hand as had kept the ledger. The invoices weren't imprinted SUPER-STAR. They weren't imprinted at all, not even with an address. They were signed *Jack Fullbright.* They listed what Dave took to be photographic, lighting, recording equipment, each piece with a serial number. Charges were added up at the foot of a far-right column. All those he saw were scrawled *paid.* He chose a few invoices from different folders, creased them, and pushed them into a pocket.

"Who the hell are you?"

He turned around, taking off the glasses. A frail-looking girl in a bikini crouched halfway down the companionway with a thin hand on the brass rail. The dying light behind her said she was blond. There was a lot of hair and it shadowed her face. She took off big, round sunglasses and came down the last of the steps. Frowning.

"What are you doing? What's that stuff? Where's Jack?"

"In the shower," Dave said. "Are you Charleen Sims?"

She didn't answer. She ran past the bar into the cabin with the beds. "Jack," she said. "There's some dude out here, looking through your stuff."

"What!" A door slammed open. Fullbright appeared in the door-way to the front cabin. He was naked and wet. A white band around his pelvis interrupted the suntan. He stood still for a second, hands on the doorframe, staring at Dave, at the carton. Be-hind him, the girl looked scared. Then Fullbright charged. A swing of his arm sent carton, ledger book, files, flying. He lunged across the bar, grabbing for Dave. Dave stepped out from behind the bar. Fullbright's long reach knocked bottles off the shelf behind the bar. The bottles hit each other and shattered on the thick rug. Gin smells rose, whiskey smells. Dave pushed his glasses into a pocket.

"Take it easy," he said.

Fullbright didn't answer. He charged again. Dave sidestepped and put out a foot. Fullbright fell over it. His momentum pitched him into the companionway. He hit the steps hard. The crash was loud. For a few seconds, he lay face down and didn't move.

"Jack!" The girl ran to him, crouched by him, put her breakable-looking hands on him. "Jack? Are you all right?"

Fullbright moaned. Slowly he pushed himself up. He turned groggily on the steps. His look at Dave was savage. Blood ran out of his nose into his moustache, down his chin, into his chest hair. He put a hand over his nose.

"Oh, my God," the girl said.

"Why don't you get him a towel?" Dave said.

"He's bleeding to death," the girl said.

Dave took her skinny arm, pulled her to her feet. She was about as weightless as a bird. He swung her toward the sleep cabin. He slapped her butt. "Make it wet and cold."

She went, making whimpering noises. A cool, salty breath of air that said night was starting came down the companionway. Dave said to Fullbright:

"That was stupid. I'd already searched the box."

"Why?" It came muffled by the covering hand.

"It looked odd to me when you got it out of your office so fast after I'd been there. I thought you moved it on my account. Naturally that made me curious about what was in it. You run your own business on the side, no?"

Fullbright took away his hand to try to speak and blood ran down his front. "Ribbons, goddamn it!" He yelled this and blood sprayed fine in the bloody light.

"Coming!" She sounded panicked.

"Strictly porno and skinflick makers," Dave said.

Fullbright shut his eyes and nodded. He leaned against the wall. His chest moved as if he'd run a mile. His color was pasty. Ribbons came with a beach towel big as a blanket. It was heavy for her to lug. She held it against herself. Water drizzled out of it down her pretty legs. It soaked the papers scattered on the rug. She sat by him on the steps and began trying to mop the blood off him. He yanked a corner of the towel away from her and wadded it against his face, moaning again. He opened his eyes and glared at Dave. The towel muffled his words.

"You practically killed me," he said.

"You tripped," Dave said. "It's never safe to run on a boat." Watching Ribbons at her inept and tearful first aid, Dave found a cigarette and lit it. He told Fullbright, "I can understand your wanting to keep your little sideline secret from your partner. He was a religious fanatic. He wouldn't like it. He also was a businessman and wouldn't like your keeping all the profits for yourself." Fullbright began to shudder. Dave went into the cabin and stripped a blanket off one of the beds. He brought it back and pushed it at Ribbons. "He's chilling. Wrap him up."

"Why don't you get out of here?" she said. But she took the blanket and began getting it around Fullbright very clumsily. "Haven't you done enough?"

"I haven't found out enough." Dave said it from back of the bar, treading carefully in all the broken glass. He found a bottle of Courvoisier that Fullbright's hysteria had spared. Glasses hung upside down from racks over the bar. He took one down and half filled it. He went back to Fullbright, crouched in front of him, gently pulled away the hand clutching the wad of towel, tipped the brandy into his mouth. His eyes were closed again. He coughed, spluttered. Opened his eyes. He pushed feebly at the glass. "Take it," Dave said. "It'll make you feel better. Guarantee."

"He's dying," Ribbons whimpered.

"Nobody dies of a broken nose," Dave said. Fullbright had the glass in his hand now and worked on the brandy by himself. Dave stood up. "What I can't understand is why you'd bother to keep it a secret from me."

"The IRS," Fullbright said. "I never paid taxes on it."

"And you thought I'd run to the Feds," Dave said.

"Why not? I don't know you. I don't know what you're nosing around about. Yes, I was scared. I thought they had Jerry's murder all wrapped up. Then you walk in and it's a whole nother ballgame." He looked sourly at the strewn wreckage of his records. "I was going to take those out to sea tomorrow and dump them."

"So Dawson doesn't connect to Spence Odum," Dave said.

"Dawson connects to Old Rugged Cross Productions," Fullbright said. "Connected. To the Salvation Army, the Methodist Overseas Mission, the Baptist Synod, the Bringing in the Sheaves Women's Auxiliary."

An ashtray was on a coffee table in front of one of the buttoned couches. The ashtray was in the shape of a ship's helm, with a shallow bowl of amber glass set into it. Dave put ashes from his cigarette there. He looked at the weepy girl. "Your name isn't Ribbons. What is it really—Charleen?"

"I don't have to tell you anything." She looked at Fullbright. "Do I have to tell him anything?"

Dave said, "Only if your name is Charleen. And, if you'd really like to be helpful, where you come from."

"From Santa Monica." She jerked her head under all that heavy blond hair. "Two miles from here. All my life. And it's not Charleen." She made a face. "Yuck. It's not just Ribbons, either. It's —get ready for this—Scarlet Ribbons. From an old Harry Belafonte record my mom had when she was about ten or something. When she grew up she was going to have a little girl and call her Scarlet Ribbons. Believe it. Then she went and married a man named Schultz. And it didn't make any difference. Her name was Hathaway. Now that would have been almost all right, right? But Scarlet Ribbons Schultz? That's too much, isn't it?"

Dave smiled. "It's quite a bit." He asked Fullbright, "Feeling better?"

Fullbright pushed the towel into Ribbons's lap and stood up, hitching the blanket around him with one hand, the other one hanging onto the empty glass. "I felt fine until you showed up. I still would the fuck like to know what you want with me."

"Dawson was sleeping with a kid about like this one." Dave nodded at Ribbons. "In a top-level apartment above the Sunset Strip. She's not there anymore. I'm looking for someone to tell me where she is."

"Jerry? Sleeping with a teenage girl?" Fullbright laughed. "You have to be out of your mind."

"I don't believe he was murdered on his street," Dave said. "I believe he was murdered in that apartment and transported across town after he was dead and dumped there for his wife to stumble over in the morning. His wife and son."

"And you think Charleen—that's the girl, right? You expected me to have her here?" Fullbright took the brandy bottle off the bar and poured another shot into his glass. To do this he had to let the blanket fall but he didn't care. He drank from the glass before he picked the blanket up again. "I don't have her here. I never had her here. I never heard of her. If Jerry was really sleeping with her, you can bet he wouldn't tell anybody, least of all me. He had his moral superiority to maintain." He grinned. Very gingerly he touched his nose. Blood had stopped coming out of it but it was swelling. So was the flesh around his eyes. And turning dark red. "That's a wild idea. I mean, the wildest."

"Somebody's got her someplace," Dave said. "Unless she was killed the same night as Dawson, as Ludwig."

"Ludwig?" Fullbright's head came forward, scowling. "Herman Ludwig, the cameraman?"

"Shotgun," Dave said. "You didn't know?"

Fullbright looked stunned. He shook his head. "They got him, then—the commies?"

"That's what his wife thinks," Dave said.

"Jesus," Fullbright whispered and drank more brandy.

Ribbons took the wet and bloody towel back to the head.

"What about Spence Odum?" Dave said. "He never mentioned this Charleen child to you?"

"I haven't talked to Spence in—hell, how long? I find him when I want to get paid. That's about it."

"Take care of yourself," Dave said, and went up the companionway into what was left of daylight.

13

The headlights of the Triumph showed cut brush heaped high next to the driveway, almost covering the mailbox. The Triumph jolted down into the yard. Where limbs had been sawed off shrubs and trees, the wounds showed white. Under the naked-looking trees, sand was heaped, sacks of cement, stacked two-by-fours, bundles of wood shingles. The headlights shone back at him, multiplied in the panes of the French doors. He wanted the natural cover back.

He yanked the wheel of the Triumph to park it and the lights gleamed off a yellow motorbike. A youth sat with his back against it. He winced in the light and stood up. He seemed to unfold forever. He had to be seven feet tall. Reedy, all knuckles, wrists, joints, he came toward the car. Clean white Levi's, clean white T-shirt, clean fair hair cut short. Dave shut off the engine. Crickets. The boy leaned down to peer inside. He looked worried.

"Mr. Brandstetter? Can I talk to you, sir?"

"Not if you're selling magazines," Dave said.

"What?" The boy sounded ready to cry. "Oh, no. No, it's important. It's about—the case you're working on. Bucky Dawson's father? The one who was murdered, you know?"

"What's your name?" Dave pushed the door handle and the boy backed a step and Dave got out of the Triumph.

"Engstrom," the boy said, "Dwight." In the dark, his voice sounded too young for the size of him. "I saw you yesterday, when you came to see Bucky, and I heard you talking to his mom. I live across the street."

"In the house with the noisy window latches," Dave said. "Come on." He headed for the cookhouse. What he took to be bricks loomed in the courtyard under the oak. He said, "How did you find me?"

"I got worried. I asked Bucky. He said it was about the insurance and if you asked me I should just tell you the same thing I told the police."

Dave found the light switch this time without guessing. "You're on the basketball team at Bethel Church, right?" He opened the refrigerator and peered into the dark. "All I've got here that's nonalcoholic is milk." He looked up into the boy's scared blue eyes. "Will milk be all right?"

"Thank you. That's very kind." Engstrom stared around him. The kitchen was plainly stranger than he liked. It made him uneasy but he didn't run. "Yes, I'm on the team. I'm not a good athlete but I'm tall."

"I noticed." Dave unwrapped a glass, rinsed it at the tap, and filled it with milk. Engstrom took it, drank from it, and left a little-kid milk line on his upper lip.

He said, "Bucky said it was Sequoia Insurance, so I called them and they gave me this address. They gave me the phone too, but no one answered."

The plastic-bagged ice cubes in the freezer compartment had clumped. Dave took the bag out and banged it on the tile counter. He put the cubes that came loose into a glass and pushed the bag away again. "And what did you say to the police?" He measured

100

gin over the ice cubes. He flavored the gin with vermouth. "That Bucky was with you in the church basement till eleven-thirty or twelve the night his father was killed?" He got olives from the refrigerator, dropped two into the drink, recapped the little bottle, shut it up in the dark again. Pushing the ice cubes clockwise with a finger, he turned to face the tall boy, eyebrows raised.

"Bucky said that was best. It wouldn't do any harm. They had the man that killed him. It would only confuse things and make a lot of useless trouble for his mother."

"But it wasn't true?" Dave tasted the drink. Warm.

"Reverend Shumate came down and said there was a phone call for him. Around nine. He went and didn't come back. I've been very—I felt bad about lying. Worried. Then when you came and started asking stuff, and Bucky was scared and begged me not to tell you anything different—well, I thought I better tell you the way it really was."

"Why not the police?" Dave lit a cigarette. "If you want to clear your conscience—they're the ones you lied to."

Dwight Engstrom's childlike face turned red. "Do I have to? I hate for them to know I lied before."

"It hardly ever works out," Dave said.

"I won't do it again," Engstrom said earnestly, "never in my life. I wouldn't have done it then for anybody else. But Bucky—I guess you don't know him too well. But Bucky would never do anything wrong."

"There aren't any human beings like that," Dave said.

"He just wanted to protect his mother," Engstrom said. "They had enough trouble already, didn't they?"

"How much is enough?" Dave said. "What did Bucky do with those three hours?"

"I don't know. I asked him. He said it didn't matter."

"It matters." Dave took jack cheese out of the fridge and cut squares off it. He held the small bright new cutting board out to the boy. "Eat. Did you get home at midnight?" Engstrom's big clean hand fumbled little cheese cubes into his mouth. "Did you see Gerald Dawson, Senior, lying dead in front of his garage doors?"

Engstrom swallowed. "No, I came home the back way."

Dave took a bite of cheese. It had bits of *jalapeño* in it. Fiery. He nodded for the boy to eat some more. Engstrom shook his head. Dave set the board down and tried his drink again. It had chilled. He said, "But it was Shumate who came to get Bucky?"

"He was back in ten minutes. Reverend Shumate, I mean. That's why practice went on so late." Engstrom gave a wry little smile. "He's a basketball freak. He never wants to quit." He finished off the milk, set the glass down with a click on the counter tiles, and looked anxious. "It'll be all right, now, will it? You won't have to tell the police I lied, will you?"

"It won't be all right," Dave said, "you know that. But I thank you for coming and telling me. It will help. Not Bucky Dawson and his mother. It will help me." He put a hand in the middle of Engstrom's long bony back and steered him to the kitchen door. "Maybe I won't have to tell the police. But if I do, you won't feel too bad about it."

"Oh, yes, I will," Engstrom said, sounding again as if he might cry. He took three steps into the darkness and turned back. "Why won't I?"

"You'll be among friends," Dave said.

His legs ached, not from the climb but from sitting on the floor at Noguchi's. Also he was a little drunk from the flame-warmed sake. But the black-lacquer surroundings had been pleasant and the food had been all right. He'd kept away from vinegar and raw fish. Mel Fleischer had been amiable enough and his young friend Makoto had been good to look at. He hadn't worn a happy coat. He'd worn torn-off Levi's and a tank top printed with the USC Trojan helmet. In the candlelight, he'd looked carved out of some fine-grained brown wood rubbed to a flawless finish. He had a terrible accent but his smile made up for it. Dave hoped he'd understood as little English as he spoke, because most of Mel's talk had been about boys he'd had before Makoto. The stories were witty even if you'd already heard them, and Dave had. But he doubted they'd inspire fidelity.

He tried the buzzer at number thirty-six but no one came, and he worked the lock with the blade from his key case again. He rolled the glass door quietly aside and didn't turn on the lamps. He used the cord to pull the curtains across and went through the place with a small flashlight. Nobody'd been here. It was all the same as before. He checked the closet again, poked around among the little shoes. He didn't know why there should be so much grit under them. You didn't pick up dirt like this cruising sidewalks, sitting in the Strip Joint, doing the boogaloo. It wasn't sand from a beach. It was soil. It looked and crumbled between his fingers like crop-growing earth.

He went back into the main room and worked the cord so the drapes came open. Out there, Los Angeles sloped sparkling to the sea. The surf sound came again from the traffic along the Strip. And there was the sound of a stereo through a wall. More than simply the thud of bass. He could almost make out the tune. He stepped past the shadowy shapes of the velveteen couches and put his ear to the wall. It was that late Billie Holliday album, the one with too much orchestra. She'd had almost no voice left by then. *I'll hold out my hand, and my heart will be in it . . .*

He pressed the buzzer next door. The glass panel was open and the music came out clear and sad. A voice yelped over it. He thought what it meant was that he was supposed to come in so he went in. The unit was the same as thirty-six except for the bulky case of one of those television sets that projects its images on a wall, and modular shelves weighed down with sound equipment, amplifier, receiver, open-reel and cassette tape decks, record player, equalizer, all of it black-faced and very new. Big black waffle-front monitor speakers hung angled from the melon-color ceiling.

A young man's shaggy head appeared over the back of a couch. The face was familiar. From TV commercials—savings-and-loan, deodorant soap, dogfood. He had a wide mouth that curled up attractively at the corners. It didn't do that now. He frowned and stood up quickly. He was wearing a shower coat in narrow rainbow stripes. A fat paperback book was in his hand. He frowned and said something the music didn't let Dave hear. Dave looked blank. The young man went to the shelves. Billie Holliday sang *You brought me violets for my furs* ... Then she wasn't singing anymore.

"That what you wanted? Too much noise?"

"It's not noise," Dave said, "and I didn't come to complain. I came to ask about the girl next door." He crossed the shag carpet to show his open wallet to the young man. "It's an insurance matter. Death claims."

"Is she dead? Is that what happened to her?"

"What makes you think something happened to her?"

The book was still in his hand. He took it to the coffee table where there was a stack of shiny books. He laid it on the stack and picked up a cigarette pack and a lighter. He offered Dave a cigarette and lit one for him and for himself. He shrugged. "She hasn't been around lately. And I always knew when she was around. Believe it."

"The walls are thin," Dave said.

"I'm not secretive and I like the view." He picked up an empty mug from the table. "She never complained about my stereo. I never complained about her tricks. A drink? Coffee? What?"

"Coffee's fine," Dave said, "if it's no trouble."

"Sit down." He went into a kitchen beyond a breakfast bar like Charleen's. Dave sat down and heard him pour coffee. "My name's Cowan, Russ Cowan." He came back with two mugs and set them down. The coffee in them steamed. "It must be interesting work." He didn't sit down.

"So must yours," Dave said.

Cowan grimaced. "Except I never know if there's going to be any more." He went back to the breakfast bar.

"I always know there'll be more," Dave said. "She brought pickups here?"

"You wouldn't think Sylvia would let her get away with that, would you?" Cowan poured brandy into a little globe glasses and came back with them. "But Sylvia concentrates on her cards. There's a lot she misses if it doesn't go on at an octagonal table." He handed Dave one of the little glasses, kept the other for himself, and sat down.

"Thank you." Dave passed the glass under his nose. It was Martel's. "Nice. When was the last time you saw the girl?"

Cowan squinched up his eyes and looked at the ceiling. "A week?" he asked himself. "No. It was longer than that." He snapped his fingers and grinned at Dave. "I know when it was." He named the date. "That's eleven days ago, right? The reason I remember is, my agent called. I had to buy him lunch at Scandia. He'd signed me for a big part in *Quincy.*"

"A good day for you." Dave set down the brandy glass and tried the coffee. It was rich and strong. "A bad day for Gerald Dawson. Somebody broke his neck."

"And that's what you're investigating?"

"He rented that unit for the girl. If Sylvia would have been upset about the tricks, think how he'd have felt. Did you ever meet him?"

"A little, dark, wiry guy in his forties? I never met him but he was in and out so much I figured he must be the one paying the bills. Who killed him? Why?"

"I was hoping you could tell me." Dave drank some more coffee and followed it with a taste of the brandy. "That's very nice. Was she noisy as usual that night? Or"—he glanced at the sound equipment—"were you listening to music?"

"I was sleeping. That was a long lunch. All afternoon. I was boozed stupid. I had a date for later." He wagged his head with a forlorn smile. "I wanted to wake up fresh and sober. Fat chance. My bedroom's next to her bedroom. All hell broke loose in there. Her yelling, him yelling, some old woman yelling."

"What time would this have been?" Dave asked.

"You bet I looked at the clock. Resentfully. You know how lousy you can feel when you wake up too soon after you pass out drunk? Early. What—eight, ten after?" He snorted a laugh, stubbed out his cigarette in a brown pottery ashtray. "I lay there thinking it was going to end soon. It didn't. So I got up and crawled into the shower. When I came out, I guess I heard the tag end of it."

"Could you make out any of the words?" Dave asked.

Cowan tilted his shaggy head, blinked thoughtfully, eyes twinkling. "Yeah, now that you mention it, I did. From the wedding service. 'For richer, for poorer, in sickness, in health.' Only not like at a wedding service. She was yelling it and she was broken up, you could tell, furious, desperate, everything." He raised his hands and wagged them.

"The girl? Charleen?"

"No, no. The old woman. Then it sounded like somebody fell down. I mean, this place is built very flimsily. I felt it in the floor under my feet. I thought I better go see. But I only got to the door there. And out this old woman comes. A big old woman, tall."

"Walking with a cane," Dave said, "dragging one foot."

"That one." Cowan nodded. "And then it settled down. I was clean but I still didn't feel good. I went back to bed. Maybe I got an hour's sleep, and then it started again. Only this time there were two men. It wasn't that loud. Except for Charleen screeching 'Get out of here and leave us alone,' I couldn't make out any words. The men didn't shout." Cowan took a cigarette from the pack Dave offered. Dave did the lighting up this time. Cowan said, "I guess I felt a little better by then. Anyway, I was curious. I heard her door slide and I went to see who this one was. A gangly dude in a suit that looked like J. C. Penney in Fresno."

"You didn't see his face?"

"I only see their backs. They have to go thataway to get to the stairs, remember?"

Dave worked on the coffee and brandy again. "What do you think was going on?"

Cowan shrugged. "She was Dawson's old lady, wasn't she? Man must've been her lawyer. Anyway, it wasn't over. Around nine-thirty, it started up again. Men shouting. I went to snoop and Dawson shoves this kid out. I mean hard. He hit that iron railing out there and I thought he'd go over it. But he didn't. Stocky kid, very black eyebrows. He was crying. He went and hammered on the door awhile but they didn't let him back in, and next time I looked, he was gone." Cowan nodded to himself, drank coffee, sipped brandy, blew out smoke. "Yeah, lively night."

"No developments beyond that?" Dave wondered. "Or did you lose interest?"

"I scrambled some eggs and watched some TV. I had a late date. My girl friend was house-sitting in Beverly Hills, kid-sitting, dog-sitting. The people were going to be home at midnight. We planned to hit the discos. So around eleven I started getting ready. And all hell broke loose next door again. I was shaving, so I didn't go look right away. But when I did, the kid was back. Charleen came running out on the gallery and he came out after her and dragged her back inside. She must have been drunk as hell. She was just barely able to stand up. He practically carried her."

"And Dawson?" Dave said. "Where was he?"

"I didn't see him," Cowan said.

14

Old nails shrieked, old lumber cracked. He lay face down, eyes shut tight, wanting to sleep again. He'd been too many places yesterday, all of them too far apart. The Triumph didn't ride easy. He felt bruised. That he could probably soak out in the shower. What wouldn't soak out were the faces, the voices, the sad facts. The trouble with life was, nobody ever got enough rehearsal. He groped out for the stereo and didn't find it. He turned his head and opened an eye. Knots in the pine wall stared at him. He pushed the power button. Harpsichord, Bach, Wanda Landowska. He blew out air, threw back the sweat-soaked sheet, sat up. He ran a hand down over his face, tottered to his feet, staggered to the bathroom.

"What a treat!" Amanda said when he came out.

He stepped back inside and took an old blue corduroy robe off a hook on the bathroom door. He put it on and tied the sash and came out again. He took the mug of coffee she offered and said, "The thing that is going to make you a success is that you get everything to happen right away. Nobody gets building materials delivered in two days. Nobody gets workmen on the job that fast."

108

He went out into the courtyard. The big speechless sons were on the roof of the front building ripping up shingles and kicking them off the eaves. Showers of dry leaves, seeds, dirt, fell with each kick. The one-armed father sat under the oak grouchily knocking old mortar off bricks with a trowel.

"Did you want it to happen later?" Amanda asked.

"Only if they invent a way to do it without sound."

"If they don't start early, they don't start." She studied him over the rim of her coffee mug. "Are you all right? I could send them away."

"No, I'm all right." From the cookhouse came the smell of bacon, the sound of bacon sizzling. He went that way. "It's the case that's all wrong. I said yesterday that if I were the man's wife and kid I'd run away."

"I remember," she said. "Have they?"

"I doubt it." Dave stopped at the cookhouse door. Delgado was in there. He looked rested and clean. He was turning bacon with a fork. Dave smelled coffee, heard the drip of it in the pot. Delgado smiled at him. It made Dave unhappy. Unhappier. He'd forgotten Delgado. He said to Amanda, "But now I *know* they should have."

She stared. "You don't mean they killed him."

"Respectability." Dave stepped into the cookhouse. "You remember respectability? No, you're too young. Everybody lived by it once. It never meant much, it hardly means anything anymore. It didn't bear any relation to reality. Today most people know that. But not everybody. Gerald Dawson found it out and it killed him. Now it's going to destroy his wife and son."

"Decency," Amanda began.

"Not decency. Respectability." Dave watched Delgado lay the bacon slices on paper toweling on the stove, watched him pour beaten eggs from a yellow bowl into a frying pan where butter sizzled. "What the neighbors think of you. Only there aren't any neighbors anymore. And if they think, they don't think about you, they think about themselves."

She gave him one of her long, thin brown cigarettes. The pack came out of a pocket in a chambray workshirt with pearl buttons. She lit it for him. "It's more widespread than you think," she said. "People pretend not, but it is."

Delgado said, "I located him for you." His glance at Dave was brief. He got busy laying toast on plates, bacon strips, spooning out the eggs. But the look was that of a kid wanting praise, needing praise, lots of it. "Nothing orthodox went far. Driver's license, I mean, that stuff." He turned and held out plates to Dave and Amanda. "But I thought about his business. And I started around places where they develop movies and record sound and that kind of thing. I didn't pick the big ones."

They went out into the heat and brightness of the morning. They trailed back across to the fencing room. They didn't sit on the bed today. They sat on the floor, backs against the wall, in a row, Amanda in the middle. Delgado looked past her, eager, pleased with himself. "I picked the little ones. And, sure enough, down Wilcox, across from the park, there's this dark little doorway kind of hidden next to one that opens into an honest-to-god shop— knitting? lamps? sandals? something. Anyway, behind the other door is a place where you can edit film and dub sound tracks and all that. Two, three rooms jammed with equipment, run by this little wall-eyed guy. And he wasn't going to give me shit." Delgado broke off, flushed, and said "Excuse me," to Amanda. He said to Dave, "Only there was this poster on the wall. A Spence Odum production, no less." Delgado washed down a big fast bite of toast with coffee.

"*All the Way Down?*" Dave asked.

"*Sisters in Leather,*" Delgado said. "A lot of pudgy broads in nothing but crash helmets and boots on big black badass motorcycles. Dikey."

"Watch it," Dave said.

"So Odum's got this place he usually shoots," Delgado said. "He runs around to locations in a white van. He doesn't pay for permits.

He shoots and runs. But the thing he calls his studio is out on the Strip. Back of a real-estate office. One room. Some producer."

"You didn't go there," Dave said.

"I banged on the door," Delgado said. "Nobody came. In the real-estate office, they never heard of Spence Odum. Talk about respectable. It could have been a church." He poked into the pocket of a very crisp white short-sleeve shirt—he must have redeemed a bundle of laundry someplace—and handed Dave a slip of paper. "There's the address."

"Thanks." Dave gave him a smile. "Well done."

"Anything else?" Delgado sounded eager.

Dave shook his head. "It's over. The son did it. Don't feel bad. You always have to chase a lot of wrong answers before you get the right one. You know that."

"Yeah," Delgado said but he sounded forlorn. "I know. What about the teenage girl—Charleen?"

"She was a witness," Dave said, "but we're not going to find her. The last time she was seen alive—if she was alive—was with Bucky."

"You said you liked it," Amanda said. "I think it's horrible. How can you go through it again and again?"

"It doesn't always turn out this depressing." Dave set his plate down, pushed to his feet, stepped over the plate, and went to where his slacks and jacket hung over a loudspeaker. He came back with his wallet and pushed into Delgado's shirt pocket a fold of fifty-dollar bills. "Pay off your motel so there'll be someplace I can get you when I need you—right?"

Delgado's face darkened. He handed back the money. "Stop acting guilty, will you? You didn't take my job. That wasn't me talking. That was Jim Beam."

Dave tucked the money into Delgado's pocket again. "I didn't say I was giving it to you. You'll earn it." He looked down at unhappy Amanda. "Forget it," he said. "I'm sorry for talking about it in front of you. Smile, okay? And go forth and destroy?"

"Just old two-by-fours," she said. "Not lives."

"Come on, now," he said. "It's not that simple."

"I'm sorry." Her smile was wan. "I didn't mean it."

He went to rummage in cartons for fresh clothes. "You meant it and it means you're a very nice lady, but I knew that anyway. I promise to wash the blood off my hands before I come back to you."

"Oh, Dave," she said. "I said I was sorry."

He headed for the bathroom to dress. Before he shut the door he said to Delgado, "Write down your address and phone number and leave it for me, okay?"

"A man's voice," Mildred Dawson said. She was no more than a tall, dim shape in the middle of a room darkened to keep out the sunlight, to keep out the heat. The room was hot and stuffy all the same. Dave wore a light knit soccer shirt, blue-and-white striped, and blue linen trousers, also light, but he was sweating. So was Bucky, sturdy and afraid in cutoff jeans, shirt open on his woolly chest. He kept sitting down and standing up again. Lyle Shumate kept murmuring to him. The woman, leaning crooked on her cane, said, "It sounded a little like Bucky. I asked who it was. He wouldn't say. All he would say was that my husband was at that apartment with that girl. Fornicating." She whispered the word.

Dave said, "Was that his expression?"

"Do you think I'd forget it?" she said. "He told me if I wanted to save him, I must come and take him away."

"Save him from what?" Dave looked at Bucky. "From death? Did he threaten to kill him?"

"From eternal damnation," she said.

"That means death, doesn't it, Reverend?" Dave peered through the shadows at the lanky man on the couch. "Didn't it occur to you that Gerald Dawson wasn't killed by Lon Tooker at all? That nobody jumped him out here on the street? That the voice on the

112

phone belonged to his killer? That you were letting the wrong man suffer, possibly even die?"

"Any of us can buy eternal damnation any day," Shumate said. "Outside the redeeming grace of our Lord and Savior Jesus Christ, there is nothing but eternal damnation."

"That's not an answer," Dave said. "That's a sermon." He swung back to Mildred Dawson. "So you went. How?"

"I have my own car," she said. "You know that. It has automatic shift. I manage."

"How did you manage the main door at the apartment complex?" Dave asked. "It locks itself. Only tenants have keys. Was your husband waiting in the lobby to let you in?"

"No. I pushed the door and it opened."

"It was braced," Bucky said, "just a crack. With a brown rubber wedge. The kind made to put under doors, you know? Only it wasn't under this one. It was stuck in the crack. At the hinge side, where it wouldn't be noticed."

"But you noticed it," Dave said.

"I was noticing everything that night," Bucky said. "Nothing like this ever happened to me before."

"It isn't going to happen again," Dave said.

"Don't be abusive." Shumate put his arm around the boy's thick shoulders. "This boy has done nothing wrong."

"You've all done wrong and you know it. Or I hope you do. If you don't, that church of yours is in trouble." He turned back to Mildred Dawson. "He'd given you the apartment number, this anonymous man on the phone? You went there, right? Up all those stairs by yourself?"

"It was a struggle," she said, "but the Lord gave me the strength. Number thirty-six, yes."

"But they weren't fornicating when you got there," Dave said, "were they? They were eating supper."

"If you know, why do you ask?" she said.

"Habit," Dave said. "I sometimes get the truth. You asked him to come home, did you?"

"I don't believe you have any authority to question us," Shumate said. "I don't believe any of us is compelled by law to tell you anything."

"You might as well practice on me," Dave said. "It will get you used to the process. A detective lieutenant from the sheriff's office named Salazar will be repeating it soon."

"Gerald wouldn't come," Mildred Dawson said. "He'd found 'happiness' and he wasn't going to give it up. No matter what it cost. Him or me or Bucky or anyone. He was completely changed. I hardly knew him." She made a bitter, mocking sound. "A little stick of a thing, and she had him bewitched."

"Did he strike you?" Dave said. "Someone fell down. My witness heard it."

"He wouldn't," she said. "It was the girl."

"So you came home and called Shumate," Dave said.

Shumate said, "He wouldn't come for me, either."

"I didn't want Bucky to know," Mildred Dawson said. "I was so ashamed. But Gerald would come for Bucky. He loved Bucky and if Bucky asked him, he'd come home. So I told Reverend Lyle to send Bucky, and Bucky went."

Dave looked at the black-browed boy. "They weren't eating when I got there," Bucky said. "They forgot to lock the door. They were naked in bed together. And he hit me. Knocked me down, hard. He picked me up and threw me out. I banged on the door and cried. He wouldn't let me back in."

"But later he did," Dave said. "Around eleven."

"What!" Bucky stood up again.

"And you tried to take him by force and you broke his neck. My witness didn't see how you got his body out of there. But he did see Charleen try to run away. He saw you drag her back into the apartment."

"He's lying!" Bucky shouted. "I wasn't there then."

114

"He thought she was drunk because she staggered. But that wasn't it, was it? You were trying to kill her. She was half dead, wasn't she? Then, when you got her back inside, she was all the way dead—just like your father."

"No!" Bucky wailed. "I didn't kill anyone."

"You couldn't burn her up like your father's dirty magazines," Dave said. "What did you do with her, Bucky?"

"She was alive when I left there. My father was alive." Bucky choked on tears. He held out his hands, begging. "You have to believe me. Please! Please!"

"His father's car was here." Shumate stood and put an arm around Bucky. "Doesn't that convince you?"

"Not that he drove it," Dave said. "Anyway, it's Salazar you have to convince." He went to the door. Bucky ignored Shumate. He stared wide-eyed at Dave. Mildred Dawson stared. Dave opened the door and went out into the heat.

15

Piñatas hung from the old black rafters of a lean-to roof above Salazar's beautiful head. They seemed to float there like animals in a Chagall painting—papier-mâché goats, burros, chickens, furred and feathered in shredded tissue paper, colors bright and clashing, red, orange, green, blue, bubble-gum pink. With flat tissue-paper eyes, they watched Indianans in Bermuda shorts and sundresses inch their way along the narrow bricked lanes between the huarache booths, sombrero booths, serape booths, the cactus-candy and woven-basket booths of Olvera Street. Mariachi music twanged and tin-trumpeted from loudspeakers. The hot air was thick with chili smells from greasy taco stands. A quartet of rouged children with paper roses in their hair and spangles on ruffled skirts danced to the music.

Behind Salazar, strings of shiny painted gourds framed a dark restaurant doorway. He sat across from Dave at a gingham-covered table and ate enchiladas, as Dave did, washing them down, as Dave did, with orange soda from thick, lukewarm bottles. "I can't arrest him. How can I arrest him?" He wiped his chin with a paper napkin. He looked like a silent-movie idol—Gilbert Roland? "Ken Barker says he was murdered on his own street in LA. Ken Barker says this porno-shop owner killed him. Now I'm supposed to come barging in and say he was killed in some apartment on the Strip. His own kid killed him?"

"His own kid admits he was there," Dave said. "Cowan saw him there."

"Cowan didn't see any murder," Salazar said.

"But nobody saw Gerald Dawson alive after that. The Medical Examiner says he was killed between ten and midnight. And Bucky lied to Barker."

Salazar shook his head and moodily poked at his refritos with his fork. "It doesn't make a murder case," he said. "All it makes is a family fight."

"Come on, now," Dave said. "You don't believe that. What's the matter? Is it the car you're worried about? Why didn't the wife, the widow, think of it afterward, get into her own car with Bucky, drive back there, so Bucky could drive Dawson's car home while she followed in her own car?"

"People get hysterical, they forget details." Glumly Salazar drank orange soda. "Even details as big as a car."

"Alone, maybe," Dave said. "A kid, especially. But he wasn't alone. His mother helped. So did the preacher. They even remembered a detail as small as the keys."

Salazar's mouth was full of pink rice. He looked his question with big, smoldering brown eyes.

"If Dawson had driven himself home and was in the process of opening the garage, the keys would have been in his hand. They weren't. Or in his pocket. Or on the street. They weren't anywhere. Lon Tooker didn't have them. I suggest you search Bucky's room."

"You're kidding." Salazar paused with a forkful of enchilada halfway to his mouth. "Why hide the stupid keys?"

117

"Because two of them fitted the Strip apartment—the street door, the door to unit thirty-six."

"Why not get rid of them and leave the car keys?" Salazar put the forkful of food into his mouth.

"Because he didn't know which they were. There would have been keys to Superstar Rentals there too. Anyway, you mentioned hysteria."

Salazar washed the food down with orange soda. "And you mentioned presence of mind. You can't have it both ways, Brandstetter. If it was like you say, he could have stripped off all the keys but the ones for the car."

"Not without prompting a lot of questions," Dave said. "It was better to take the chance of the cops assuming the killer had taken the whole bunch and thrown them away."

"And why didn't he?" Salazar said.

"Because Bucky drove the car and he still has them."

Salazar cocked an eyebrow, pressed his mouth tight, shook his head. "Barker says you're very, very smart. But there are different kinds of smart, aren't there? What I hear in all this is the rattle of a cash register. You're trying to save that insurance company that hired you money. Tooker can't help you. But the widow and orphan can, right?"

"Tooker didn't have anything to do with this."

"What about the horse stuff on the deceased's clothes?"

"Check the closet in unit thirty-six," Dave said, "the shoes there, the dirt on the floor."

"Yeah, unit thirty-six." Salazar brushed a fly away from the guacamole bowl. "What did the widow and the kid care about unit thirty-six?"

"They didn't care about anything else," Dave said. "If you can't grasp that, no wonder you don't believe me. Let me explain it to you one more time. What they were trying to do by losing the keys to the place, bringing the body away from there, bringing the car away from there, wasn't just to avoid a charge of murder one. They

118

wanted it to look as if Gerald R. Dawson had never set foot in that apartment, never touched that girl. To them, the Strip is Sodom and Gomorrah. Gerald R. Dawson was a saint."

Salazar didn't say anything. He only looked. He dipped a chip of fried tortilla into the guacamole, put it into his mouth, and munched. He licked his fingers.

Dave said, "They wanted the police, the *Times,* the *Examiner,* the 'Eyewitness News', everybody, the world, to think their beloved husband and father was, in death as in life, the same upright and unsullied crusader for Christ they'd always believed he was. Hell, Bucky showed me that the first morning I saw him. He claimed those porno magazines he was burning were his. They weren't. His father had ripped them off at Lon Tooker's shop. But Bucky didn't care about bringing what his unreal little world would call disgrace on himself. No matter what it cost him—he was going to protect his father's image."

"Even if he had to kill him to do it." Salazar picked up his orange-soda bottle and set it down again. He laughed. Not happily. Hopelessly. "Wow, that is weird, Brandstetter. You know that, don't you? Weird."

"If your lab people will take their little vacuum cleaners and go over that apartment," Dave said, "you'll see it's not all that weird. Mrs. Dawson wasn't able to save her husband from hellfire. Lyle Shumate was his minister and friend but he failed. Bucky failed, and he couldn't accept it. Maybe he talked it over with mama, maybe not. But he went back there and tried to use force and something went wrong. Bucky claimed his dad couldn't fight but he must have tried. Anyway, he ended up dead."

"Weird," Salazar said again, and stacked his dishes. "I mean, even if you accept it as accidental—it's still weird. And, anyway, what about the girl? You've been in that unit. Her body's not there. Where is she?"

"Damned if I know." Dave got off the creaky wooden chair. "I can't see Bucky killing her in cold blood." He picked up the check, took out his glasses, and read it. "But where did she go? I keep seeing twiggy little girls under haystacks of hair and hoping they're her. They never are." He tucked the glasses away. "I don't find Bucky easy to believe but I can't shake the feeling she's still alive."

"Not if he killed his old man." Salazar stood up and stretched. His fists struck the piñatas. They swung and jostled each other, rustling. "Not if she saw him do it." He steadied the piñatas.

Ducking under their trailing fringes, Dave went down through the dark doorway into the restaurant and paid the check. When he came back outside, Salazar was tossing dimes and quarters to the dancing children. Dave said to him:

"Check out that apartment, please?"

"Barker won't like it," Salazar said.

"It will be one less case for him to worry about."

Hot daylight came down through the roof into the big room. Sawdust drifted in the shafts. Above, the shadows of the speechless sons moved. Their shoes clunked and shuffled. Saws whined, hammers banged. Amanda stood looking up, shading her eyes ·with a hand and trying to talk over the racket. Beside her stood Ken Barker. He nodded. He pointed. His bulk made Amanda look very small and fragile. With *homo sapiens,* nature was still building experimental models. They could have represented different species. He crossed the sawdusty floor to stand beside them. Barker turned him a sour look. Through the carpentery noises he said:

"You're making yourself damned unpopular."

"I can't hear you," Dave lied. He kissed Amanda's forehead and led Barker out into the courtyard, where grouchy one-armed dad still sat in the speckled shade of the big oak, methodically clamping bricks between his knees and whacking mortar off them with his trowel. Amanda went to him and they conferred. Dave led Barker into the cookhouse, got beer from the refrigerator, pried off the caps, and handed a bottle to Barker. "Salazar drinks orange soda pop with his Mexican food. I thought I better have as clear a head as he had."

"Mrs. Dawson is getting out a restraining order against you," Barker said. "She told me and the DA you were harassing her and accusing her son of murder. I don't have to ask you if it's true. I know you."

Dave leaned against the sink counter and told him the whole long story. He was getting bored with it now. Also uneasy. There was a warped, pathetic kind of logic to Bucky's killing his father. An inevitability. Dawson had set standards he couldn't live by himself. His son was too young yet to have begun to doubt them. The thing had been building from the day Bucky was born. But not Charleen's death. They made an awkward match. He didn't put this into words for Barker. He finished his Dos Equis and his story. "There's no restraining order against you. Go through Bucky's room. You'll find those keys."

Barker dug into a pocket. He held up keys on a small bright ring that dangled off a stiff leather fob. Dave put out a hand for them. Barker dropped them into his hand. JESUS SAVES was stamped into the fob. There had been gilt in the letters once. It had almost all rubbed off.

"Where did you get them? Not from Tooker."

Barker's smile was ironic. "Bucky. This morning. After your visit, he thought it was time to tell the truth, the whole truth. He and his mother did go to the Strip to collect dad's car—but in the morning, after she found the body, before she phoned us."

"Meaning they didn't know he was dead till then?"

"You got it." Barker set his empty bottle down on the cold stove, opened the refrigerator, brought out two full bottles. He stretched an arm past Dave for the opener on the counter. The bottles went *fft!* when he uncapped them. He handed one to Dave and tilted one up himself.

"Why isn't that just another lie?" Dave said.

121

"Because Bucky remembered a witness. A black in a starchy security uniform who's too old to care about sleeping anymore and who looks after Sylvia Katzman's underground garage. He isn't too good at standing around these days." Barker reached into Dave's shirt pocket for a cigarette and let Dave light it for him. "So he parks his 1962 Corvair right next to the driveway on the street. And he sits in it. Until some tenant slopes in. Then he gets out and looks alert and protective with that big revolver on his hip until they leave the garage. Then he gets back into his car. He can see a lot from there. Not just who drives in, but anyone who walks up the stairs to the front door. He saw Mildred Dawson around eight, Lyle Shumate around nine, Bucky around ten. Come and go. He saw Bucky again when he came to fetch his father's car, a little after dawn next morning. They even exchanged some words about it."

"But he didn't see Bucky a second time the night of the murder?" Dave lit a cigarette for himself. "At eleven?"

"Negative," Barker said. "And never any Charleen—not at any time. Or any Gerald Dawson—dead or alive." Barker went and leaned in the doorway, gazing across the courtyard at the stolid sons on the front roof. He blew away tobacco smoke. It didn't drift much. The air was still. "Of course, he has to go to the toilet. The old prostate isn't what it once was. He could have missed Bucky coming back and carrying out two dead bodies. He doesn't think so. And neither do I."

"We know where Dawson's body went," Dave said. "but not Charleen's. It's not in her apartment—I've been there. But Cowan saw her try to run away and saw Bucky drag her back inside. And that's the last anyone ever saw of her." He frowned to himself. "She must have been hurt. She wasn't drunk. There were no liquor bottles in the place."

Barker turned and drank beer and studied him. "You know, you sound shaky. You're always on target. On this, you're missing all over the place. What is it? No ground under your feet? I knew you meant a lot to Medallion. I didn't think Medallion meant that much to you. You're all of a sudden insecure, right?"

"Forget it," Dave said disgustedly. "I make mistakes all the time. You know that. What did Salazar do—only tell me he'd look at that apartment?"

"He's got a team there," Barker said. "I happened to stumble across him. But Dawson wasn't killed there, and you know it." He cocked his head. "You've been through the place. You'd have found the signs, wouldn't you? He died of a broken neck. Broken neck, strangulation, suffocation—ninety-nine times out of a hundred, the muscles that control the bladder and bowels let go. They had let go, Dave."

"When you got to the body, yes," Dave said. "More than six hours afterward. In hot weather, that's normal. Ninety-nine times out of a hundred is a sloppy figure."

Amanda came to the door. "Ah-ha! Do I get beer too?"

"In judicial hangings, where the neck is broken," Barker said, "it's a hundred percent."

"In judicial hangings," Dave said, "there's anxiety beforehand, there are nerves at work. Dawson wasn't expecting his neck to be broken."

"Dear God." Amanda ducked in past Barker, peered into the dark refrigerator, and brought out the cardboard carton the Dos Equis had come in. It was empty. She said in a faint, wavery voice, trying to smile, "Time to go storeside."

"I'll go." Dave took a step.

"No, no. You two stay and have your cheerful little chat." She looked pale. "I think I'd like to miss it."

"I'm sorry all over again," Dave said.

Barker asked, "Did I say something wrong?"

Amanda gave her head a wan little shake. "It comes with the territory," she said, and fled. But she came running back, breathless, after a moment. "I forgot. Someone called Randy Van has been on the phone for you. Strange voice. Would it be a boy type or a girl type?"

"He hasn't made up his mind yet," Dave said. She looked blank and went away, and Dave told Barker, "Anyway, Tooker can go back to his horses."

"Not if Dawson was killed in front of his house," Barker said. "And I still think he was."

Dave shook his head. "That old black man was asleep."

16

The wig was different and so was the costume, if costume wasn't an unfair word. The wig was brown with sunny streaks in it, and the dress was shirtmaker, beige, twill, with agate-color buttons. The handbag lying on the bar matched. So did the big shoes, heels hooked over the braces of the bar stool. Nail polish and lipstick were red-orange this time. But nothing was different about the smile. It said Dave was welcome, more than welcome.

The sunlight was slivered by the bamboo blinds on the windows again. There were fewer agents and lawyers and clients in the room, and at the far end of it no one fiddled with the musical instruments on the bandstand. Dave took the stool next to Randy's and looked at the drink he was holding.

"Margarita," Randy said. "Will you?"

"Dos Equis," Dave told the coveralled bartender. He said to Randy, "So Odum lied. He does know Charleen."

"She never worked in any of his pictures," Randy said, "but she was going to."

" 'Was'?" Dave said. The bottle came and a cold, wet glass. "He changed his plans?"

" 'Is', then," Randy said. "I only meant it hasn't happened. He's writing a script for her. He showed me her photo. I said, 'Why, in God's name?' And he said it was a favor for a friend."

"Photo?" Dave said.

Randy upended the handsome purse. Out came cigarettes, lighter, lipstick, coins, a rattle of keys. The big male hand with the scrupulously female nails pushed a glossy snapshot along the bar at Dave. It looked as if it had been taken in a motel room. There was something wrong about the light—he wasn't sure what. She was naked and she really did look twelve years old. The obscene pose was pathetic. He raised eyebrows at Randy. "What friend?"

"Jack Fullbright," Randy said. "I think he took the picture."

"Odum parts easily with things to you," Dave said. "Things and information."

Randy licked salt off the edge of the margarita glass. "We've been close. We still are, every now and then. He likes boys who dress up in women's clothes. I told you that. He's warm and funny and kind."

"And not everybody likes boys who dress up in women's clothes," Dave said. "And all boys who dress up in women's clothes don't like fat, fiftyish pornographers."

"It's symbiosis," Randy said. He batted his false eyelashes at Dave and swallowed delicately from his drink. "Is that the right word? Or do I want 'exploitation'?"

"What's Fullbright doing for him?" Dave drank beer. He felt big, heavy, awkward. Every move he made seemed like an act, a fake. His voice sounded too deep. It couldn't be sad. He'd never wanted to wear a dress. It had to be funny. He bit his lip to keep from laughing. "Or had Fullbright already done this favor?"

"He's going to let Spence have all the equipment he needs free," Randy said. "What's funny?"

"You make me feel like Jack Youngblood," Dave said.

"And who might that be?" Randy tilted his head.

"A man who knocks people down on football fields."

Randy shrugged. "If you're butch, you're butch." He made his laugh giddy and patted his wig. "But football is not my kind of contact sport."

"When you were playing your kind with Odum," Dave said, "did he tell you why Fullbright wanted this favor?"

The margarita glass was empty. Randy pushed it to the back edge of the bar and lifted his chin to the bartender. "I suppose to keep the girl happy." Randy peered at the snapshot. He turned it toward himself. "Though I honestly can't think why."

"I can't, either," Dave said. "He's got a different little package of female bones now. Probably has twenty a year. I'd bet on it. What kind of script?"

"He's the one with the boat?" Randy's new drink came with a neat frosting of salt around its rim. He took a ladylike sip and chose a cigarette and pushed the pack at Dave. "Boats are sexy." Dave lit the cigarettes with his manly steel lighter, grinning again. Randy said, "The script? Something about a schoolgirl and her dikey gym teacher and the gym teacher's horny boyfriend. Who knows?"

"It sounds confused," Dave said.

"It'll be funny," Randy said. "That's why he can't make any money. The creeps that want to see sex movies don't want to laugh, and he keeps putting all these laughs in. It's the only way he can stand making the things. His problem is, he's got too many brains."

"It's not brainy to lie," Dave said. He watched a scarecrow youth at the end of the bar pull music sheets out of an attaché case and lay them in front of a plump man in a Cardin suit. "No, I wouldn't give you a dollar for his brains and Fullbright's in one package—one very small package." He looked at his watch. "How come you're not doing your Bertha-the-Sewing-Machine-Girl routine?"

"Because the immigration people are always rounding up the illegals and tossing them back over the fence, right? And it takes

127

time for them to fix it up with the coyotes to get back in again, right? And Morry Steinberg's sweatshop gets very vacant during those periods. And however illegal Randy Van may be in however many ways, he, she, or it was born right here in the good old USA. Do you know Mitchell, South Dakota?"

"No, but don't hum a few bars for me," Dave said.

"Funny," Randy Van said. "Anyhow, when every other machine in the place is gathering dust, Randy's up there whipping out dem new blue jeans. So when I ask for time off, Morry never complains." He cocked a jaunty eyebrow at Dave and rocked his head. The hand that held the cigarette was bent far back at the wrist. "And today, I thought it would be fun to play Nora Charles, you know? Myrna Loy?"

"Odum is going to hate you," Dave said.

"Why? He didn't hurt anybody. And you're not going to hurt him." But the frivolity was gone. Randy looked at Dave anxiously. "You aren't, are you?"

"Earlier today, I'd have said no." Dave scowled at the brown bottle as he poured the last beer out of it. He shook his head, drank some of the beer. "Now I wonder." He looked gravely into the chorus-boy face with its thick coat of makeup. "That's what it means to be Nick Charles. A case makes perfect sense at noon. By one o'clock it makes no sense at all. But one thing I am sure of. This little girl"—he tapped the murky photograph—"was in the middle of it. And still is—alive or dead."

"Dead?" Randy forgot about his voice. It came out baritone. He cleared his throat and said, "Dead?" again, up an octave.

"Maybe, maybe not. You were in Spence Odum's living quarters, am I right? Any signs of her there?"

Randy laughed. "His living quarters are half wardrobe department, half prop room. Also carpenter shop. Also film-editing department. Also projection room. It's pure chaos. You could hide an elephant there. I didn't see any sign of her, no. I can't picture

Spence hiding a girl there, not a real, honest-to-God girl. Why would he?"

"Why would he lie to me and say he never heard of her?" Dave picked up the margarita glass and put it into Randy's hand. "Was he with you when Herman Ludwig was shot?"

"Of course. I told you—Spence was the one who sent me to find him." Randy gulped the rest of the margarita and set the glass down. "You don't think Spence killed him!" He began shoving the junk back into the handbag. "Spence couldn't step on a bug. He'd have nightmares of guilt, waking and sleeping. He wouldn't be able to eat, wouldn't be able to face people. You don't know him. He's very sensitive." Randy worked the catch on the handbag flap. "He can't even bear to hurt people's feelings. Pick up a gun and kill a human being? Even somebody he hated he couldn't do that to. And he was crazy about Herman."

"He's got a streak someplace that isn't nice," Dave said. "What about the man with his throat slit?"

"In the barber chair? That's a dummy, a joke."

"Somebody's hiding her." Dave got off the stool. "Let's go see whether he can tell the truth today."

"He's out in the van, doing location stuff," Randy said. "That's why I've got this time. I'm not in any outdoor shots. The makeup makes me sweat too much. My identity runs."

"He'll be back when it gets dark?"

Dave didn't hear Randy's answer because Mittelnacht came in at the sun-bright door. Outside it, the same suntanned youngsters were eating fancyburgers in the polluted heat. The same Peter Frampton record was yelling at them. Mittelnacht wore black glasses. A tank top dyed a dozen runny colors covered his skinny torso. The slept-in black jeans were the same. Today they were tucked into black cowboy boots. He headed for the black bandstand in the corner and Dave said to Randy, "Excuse me a minute," slid the photograph off the bar, and went after Mittelnacht. He caught up with him between empty tables. Mittelnacht took off the black glasses. His hair was lank. He smelled of baby-oil shampoo. "It's you," he said. "What's this?"

"You tell me," Dave said. "It's supposed to be Charleen."

"It is. Only where did you get it? Wow." His tone and the little brief smile that went with it were marveling. "What the fuck was she into? You know what this is, man?"

"I don't understand the question," Dave said.

"Some private eye," Mittelnacht said.

Dave took the photo back from him and studied it. "Infrared," he said. "Only to what point? Why would she pose in the dark? Was she shy?"

"Hell, she loved having her picture taken. It was a drag. Go to the beach, she'd spend twenty bucks and half a day in those take-your-own-portrait booths."

"Not this kind of portrait," Dave said.

"I've got some like that. On Polaroid. It's got a gizmo so we could appear together."

"Fully clothed, no doubt," Dave said.

Mittelnacht grinned. "Bare ass and banging."

"Somebody was with her," Dave said. "There have to be more of these pictures, a whole set, and in the rest, she's not alone. It was a setup. A dark motel room. Just her and some unsuspecting man. And a hidden photographer." He looked at Mittelnacht. "I hope you hung onto those Polaroids."

"Blackmail." Mittelnacht looked sober. "I'll get them back before I do a record that hits the charts. You bet your ass I will." His forehead wrinkled. "You didn't find her, yet? That Odum character didn't know where she was?"

"He didn't say so," Dave said. "But I'm going to ask him again tonight. If I find her, I'll try to get your pictures back for you."

"What's going on?" Randy came to them.

Mittelnacht looked him up and down doubtfully.

Dave said, "Mittelnacht, Randy Van."

They made indifferent noises. Mittelnacht said to Dave, "You really think she's alive?"

"Nobody's proved otherwise," Dave said, "and I need her to answer questions. If I can't find her, a boy that killed his own father is going to get away with it, and a man that never hurt anyone is going to end up on death row. So I have to believe she's alive, don't I?" He turned to Randy. "Do you like to ride horses?"

"Have they got sidesaddles?" Randy asked.

"Probably not. You can change. We'll stop by your place."

"I love the stopping-by-my-place idea," Randy said. "But not to change. I don't look right in britches."

"You never know till you try," Dave said. "Ah, the hell with it. We'll stop at a supermarket instead."

"What for?" Randy asked.

"Apples. If you won't exercise them, you can feed them, all right?" He lifted a hand to Mittelnacht. "Don't forget—if you see her, phone me."

Mittelnacht wasn't listening. He was staring hard at Randy. He said to Dave, "I don't think that's a girl."

"Ho-hum," Randy said.

17

It was up one of those narrow, crooked old Topanga roads that floods out in winter. Big sycamores dense with sunny green leafage leaned white trunks over a creek where the water ran summer-shallow among bleached boulders. The Triumph crossed a tough little new cement bridge. From mossy rocks beneath it, a fishing raccoon looked up. A plump gray quail led a crooked string of young across the road and into brush. Mule deer swiveled big ears at them from a clump of live oaks.

The human habitations here were mostly old and shacky. Rickety automobiles and dusty pickup trucks with camper shells waited beside them. Horses browsed by barbwire fences or found shade under corrugated plastic roofs held up by out-of-plumb four-by-fours. Their tails swished off flies. Dogs bolted into the road and chased the car, barking cheerfully. Dave kept reading tin mailboxes. The one that read TOOKER was neatly enameled white, a little housie, with the name punched out of metal along the roof peak and, topping it, a sheet-metal cutout of a bowlegged cowboy with Stetson and guitar. The old rail fence was fresh white.

The Triumph went up a drive of white gravel. The house was rickety bat-and-board but fresh white also. Fist-size rocks had been whitewashed and enclosed bright flowerbeds—nasturtiums, orange, yellow, Indian red. He parked between the Mercedes and a hard-used estate wagon, probably Tooker's. When he switched off the Triumph, he heard the slow tap of typewriter keys. At the side of the house, a deck was built around the trunk of an old pepper tree. Under the tree sat Karen Shiflett. A toy-red portable typewriter was in front of her on a TV eating table made of a wooden tray on tubular tin legs. At her bare feet were a box of envelopes and a stack of multigraphed letters. She bent close to the typewriter, peering nearsightedly. She poked the keys, studied an address book, poked the keys again. She didn't look up until Dave made a noise, setting down the carton of apples.

"Oh, hi! Where did you come from?"

Dave looked up the slope behind the house. Twenty yards off, half a dozen palominos fed on strewn hay in a white-railed paddock. Their coats shone golden, their manes and tails cream white. The paddock was half shadowed by a gaunt stable, open in front, sided and backed in vertical slats. Inside the stable moved the stick figure of the pimply kid from Keyhole Books. He looked healthier out here. When he stepped into the sunlight with a saddle blanket, his long yellow hair gleamed. He wore a green satin cowboy shirt, jeans, cowboy boots. Smoothing the blanket over the back of one of the horses, he stared down at Dave and Randy for a minute, then went back into the shadows of the barn.

"What happened to your horse sale?" Dave asked.

"Lon said no." She sighed and set aside the flimsy table that held the typewriter. She stood up and put out a hand to Randy. "Hi," she said. "I'm Karen Shiflett."

"Sorry," Dave said. "Randy Van."

"Nice to know you." Randy sounded faint and forlorn. Karen was wearing one of Lon Tooker's shirts again, knotted under her pert breasts again. Randy was eyeing those breasts. With thoughtful sadness. Karen turned for the aluminum screen door that opened from the house to the deck. She wore drawstring trousers of thin Indian cotton. Her neat little butt moved saucily inside them. Dave heard Randy sigh.

"Beer?" Karen asked. "Or lemonade?"

"Maybe with tequila?" Randy asked.

"No problem." Karen raised eyebrows at Dave.

"Beer, thanks," he said.

"He didn't murder anybody," she said when she came out with a painted Mexican tray, glasses of lemonade, a tequila bottle, a can of Coors, and a basket of corn chips. "So he doesn't need any defense." She set the tray down on the redwood bench that edged the deck. "So it isn't going to cost him anything. So don't sell the horses." She put herself on the bench next to the tray and held out Dave's beer to him. She patted the bench on the other side of the tray and said to Randy, "I'll let you put in the fire-water, okay?"

"Lovely." Randy sat down, laid his handbag aside, took up the lemonade glass, and swallowed from it deeply. He set the glass down, uncorked the tequila bottle, and laced the drink back up to the rim of the glass. Karen watched him interestedly, watched him recork the tequila, then looked up at Dave, squinting a little because of the sun through the pepper tree. "I told you Lon was a child."

"Maybe not." Dave took a blank envelope from the box and walked to the edge of the deck. He'd heard the paddock gate creak, the rattle of its latch. He heard the clop of hoofs. One of the palominos was coming downhill, the kid on its back, swaying in a tooled leather saddle. Dave vaulted the deck rail and climbed to the edge of the path. The kid reined in the horse. It looked at Dave with gentle eyes, blew softly through its big, velvety nostrils, turned its head away with a shake that rattled bit and bridle. "Do me a favor," Dave asked the kid. He held out the envelope to him. The kid swung down out of the saddle. "Scrape one of his feet a little," Dave said, "and put the scrapings into this for me."

"What for?" The kid took the envelope, blinked at it, fingered its smoothness, looked at Dave. "Some way it's going to help Lon?"

"If I hadn't thought so," Dave said, "would I have driven clear the hell out here?"

"I don't know why you want to help him," the kid said.

"He's taking up a jail cell," Dave said, "that rightfully belongs to the beneficiary of Gerald Dawson's insurance policy."

"You're trying to save your company money."

"You've got it," Dave said.

The kid shrugged. He let the horse's reins hang. It didn't offer to go anywhere. The kid put a shoulder against its glossy ribcage, bent, tapped the near fetlock. The horse lifted its foot. The kid used a twig to pry debris from the hoof. The horse put the hoof down again, took a step away and stopped. The kid picked up the debris from the path and tucked it into the envelope. He handed the envelope back to Dave. "I guess that's why they pay you," he said. "Hell, I could have thought of it and I didn't. It's going to show the horse stuff on Dawson's clothes didn't come from here, isn't it?"

"Hold the thought," Dave said, and put the envelope into a pocket. He turned back toward the house. "Thanks."

"You want to ride?" the kid said. "Your girl want to ride? They all need exercise. Karen's busy. And my ass is about worn out."

"Raincheck?" Dave said. "I want to get this to a lab."

"Don't wait too long." The kid swung back into the saddle. "They could starve to death."

"Not for apples," Dave said. "I brought a box."

"Beautiful," the kid said, and nudged the horse in the ribs with his heels. It ambled toward the road. "Lon better get his ass back here, that's all I know."

Dave returned to the deck. Karen and Randy weren't there. A breeze came from somewhere. Dry red berries pattered down from the pepper tree. The top sheets from the multigraphed stack slithered across the planks. He picked them up, glanced at them, laid them back on the stack and weighted the stack with a little green plastic pot that held a flowering cactus. He went into the house. The walls were paneled in fake birch. Paintings hung on them— little children with huge eyes, holding birds and small wild animals. A reel-to-reel tape recorder turned. A good-hearted, off-key bass voice, backed by instruction-book-one guitar chords, sang about saving the whales from the factory ships. Karen and Randy gazed at the pictures. Randy was cooing over them and downing lemonade. The tequila bottle was in his other hand. The cork was missing. He kept tilting the bottle over the ice cubes.

"We have to go," Dave said. Out on the deck again, he nodded at the multigraphed pages and the blank envelopes. "Trying to raise a defense fund?"

"Talk about hoping against hope!" Karen dropped dismally onto the bench again and wearily pulled the typewriter to her. "The creeps that came to that store wouldn't defend their own mothers —if they had mothers, which I seriously doubt. But"—she lifted her hands and let them fall—"it's the only mailing list I've got, that and a few Sierra Club buddies. I had to do something. He won't do anything." She looked up at Dave with tears in her eyes. "You saw his pictures. He painted those himself. I know they're lousy, but they're sweet. You heard that song. He's written a lot of songs like that. How could this thing happen to somebody like Lonny? How could he be so unlucky?"

"He's not so unlucky," Dave said. "He's got a friend."

In the Triumph, skidding and buzzing back down the canyon, beginning to meet upcoming cars now, people off work early, the start of the home-going rush, Randy sat silent, face turned away, gazing out the open window at the sunlight and shadows down the woodsy creekbed. The wind fluttered the neat, sun-streaked wig. He didn't seem to notice. Dave said, "Tequila got your tongue?"

Randy looked at him bleakly. "God, to have a body like that!"

"What's supposed to be wrong with the one you've got?" Dave asked. "It looks fine to me."

"It came from the wrong outfitter," Randy said.

18

The big brick room was blacked out again. This time, the lone shaft of light burned down on a sheeted body on a high table. Standing just inside the light were Spence Odum, wearing a false walrus moustache and a London bobby's outfit, and the man in tweeds with the deerstalker cap. The camera and the kid who operated it were silhouetted this side of the staring light. The camera whirred. Odum, hamming fear and trembling, slowly raised the sheet on the side away from the camera. He flinched at what he saw and turned his face aside. The man in the deerstalker cap opened his eyes wide and registered horror.

"Hold the expression," Odum said through unmoving lips. "Camera—zoom in on him tight and wait." The camera kept on whirring. "Okay," Odum said. "Cut. Turn on the lights."

The lights came on and the boy with the Adam's apple threw off the sheet and sat up. "I'm a star," he said, and jumped down off the table. He had on only jockey shorts. He kicked into jeans, flapped into a shirt.

"Quite fucked to death!" Odum laughed.

"What a way to go," the boy said.

"Where the hell have you been?" Odum sounded like an outraged parent. He was asking Randy, who stood with Dave just inside the door, next to the washrooms. "And what the hell do you want?" This he said to Dave. He came to them, walrus moustache bristling, billy club swinging at his belt. "I'm trying, for Chrissake, to get a cheap, trashy movie in the cans here." To Randy: "I needed you." To Dave: "You I didn't need."

"He doesn't take me to Fatburger," Randy said. "He takes me to places with tablecloths, where the waiters wear velvet jackets, and I can't pronounce the names on the menu, and the check is fifty dollars."

"Yes, but is it art?" Odum said. "I give you a chance to act, to express your deepest feelings. I offer you immortality. And you talk about food."

"I want to talk about murder," Dave said.

"Later." Odum swung away. "Harold? Junie? Bedtime." He went toward the corner with the shiny brass sleeping arrangement and the wallpaper. "Inspector Hardcock? You get outside the window, please."

The tweedy man, pipe in his teeth, leafed over a script. "Page forty? 'Registers shock, amazement, delight, pops eyes, licks lips'?"

"Did I write that?" Odum said. "Beautiful prose."

The naked boy and girl trudged to the bed. Junie reached for the gold velour coverlet.

"Don't touch that. Are you cold or something? You don't get under the covers, for Godsake. You're not doing this for love and human warmth. You're doing it for the camera. Anyway, there aren't any sheets on there."

"Cheap, cheap!" chanted the camera boy, the sound boy, the prop boy.

"Set the camera low so you can shoot over them while they writhe around erotically," Odum said, "and aim it at Hardcock's face in the window, okay?" He turned back suddenly and bumped into Dave, who had followed him. "What did you say you want?"

"First, you lied to me about Charleen Sims," Dave said. "You signed her for a picture. You're writing the script. You even have a photo of her. You know who she is and you knew it when I asked you before. Where is she?"

"I saw her once, yes," Odum said. "How important could that be? You looked like trouble. I don't need it."

"It was important to Gerald Dawson," Dave said. "The murdered man I mentioned? Why don't you tell me where exactly you fit in this?"

"I don't fit anywhere," Odum said. "I am completely out of it. The girl's gone? Great. I promised Jack Fullbright I'd star her in a picture. He promised he'd let me have raw film and equipment, no charge. He wanted her. I guess that was her price. I didn't object. I had this idea for a sexpot schoolgirl flick. They're doing good business in the cities these days. I'm sick of the farm-town mentality." He frowned under the little bill of the domed bobby's helmet. "Did you ask Fullbright where she is?"

"He claims he never saw her," Dave said, "never heard of her, never came near her."

"What? It was him who brought her here. What the hell does he mean?" Odum took a step backward. "Oh, now, wait. That son of a bitch. Did he send you here tonight?"

"You see?" Dave said. "You do fit into this, don't you? And tightly, too. Where is she, Odum?"

"No, I swear. Fullbright brought her in here and put his proposition to me and I said okay and I never saw her again. It didn't surprise me. I asked him for time. To raise the money. To write the script."

"She wasn't sleeping with Fullbright," Dave said. "She was sleeping with Dawson. She was with him when he was killed. Now, what do you know about Dawson?"

"He was a religious maniac," Odum said.

Junie and Harold were sitting side by side on the bed, like good

140

children waiting for their bath. Their nakedness made them look more innocent than children. Junie said, "Wasn't he the one that came in and ripped down the sets and threw stuff around?"

"When was this?" Dave asked.

"Who knows?" Odum shrugged big, soft, round shoulders inside the bulky bobby's jacket. "This was a sinkhole of vice and corruption."

"A stench in the nostrils of decent people." Harold went past them into a washroom and came out with two cans of Coke. "A plague spot of filth, an open sore."

"Jesus was coming," Junie said, "with a flaming sword."

"Not a spray can of Lysol?" Randy said. "When is he due? I'd like to look my best."

"The little man didn't give us a date," Junie said. Harold sat down beside her and handed her a Coke.

"Funny voice," Odum said. "He wanted to roar, but the madder he got, the more strangled he sounded."

"You couldn't stop him?" Dave asked.

"Spence ran and hid in the van," Harold said.

"I wanted a different perspective," Odum said. "He wasn't having his stuff used to make dirty movies. He hauled it all out of here —lights, cameras, the works. He was throwing it into the Superstar truck when Fullbright drove up. They had a big brawl, pushing, yelling, grabbing. Dawson threatened him all over the place. The police. The IRS. I don't know what all. Fullbright looked pretty sick. Dawson slammed the truck doors and took off."

"No words about Charleen?" Dave asked.

"You've got a one-track mind," Odum said. "Look, can I shoot my picture now, please?"

"Losing your sets must have slowed you down."

"Fullbright was back the next morning. With the equipment. He knocked the damages off the bill and he gave me cash to cover the extra day's studio rent. He apologized. I thought he meant it. Now suddenly he's trying to wreck me."

141

"He isn't," Dave said. "He never mentioned his deal with you. He claims he hasn't seen you in weeks."

"He hasn't," Odum said, "and neither has the girl. I wasn't mixed up with her. The only kind of girls I'm interested in turn out to be boys when they take their clothes off." Maybe it would have sounded funny anyway. It certainly sounded funny coming from a big, stolid symbol of British law and order. The only thing that saved it was that the uniform smelled of mothballs. "Fullbright was mixed up with her—that I can tell you. You can tell me Dawson was mixed up with her. I wasn't. I don't want any part of it."

"I don't know yet what Fullbright's part was," Dave said. "But Dawson's was to die. And so was yours."

"What?" Odum went pale. His big pudgy fingers shook as they worked loose the buckle on his chin strap. He took off the helmet. His hair sprang up frizzy again. He half turned away his head, watching Dave from the corners of his eyes. "What are you trying to say?"

"That Herman Ludwig was killed by mistake," Dave said. "Did you two ever stand and look into a mirror together? That parking lot out there is dark. Somebody was waiting in the dark with a shotgun. The same somebody who killed Gerald Dawson. On the same night. He saw a big, overweight, middle-aged man with thick hair standing up all over his head come out that door"—Dave pointed—"and he thought it was you, and he blew Herman Ludwig's brains out."

"No." Odum touched his lips with his tongue. He swallowed. His voice came hoarse, stammering. "It—it was the—the communists. From Hungary. He was always talking—talking about how they were following him, trying to kill him."

"The same night Dawson was killed? Dawson, who, like you, was a friend of Charleen Sims—if friend is the word? You see why I seem to have a one-track mind? You see why I have to find her?"

"If whoever it was tried to kill me for messing with her," Spence Odum said, "he had the wrong man. I swear to you I never saw

142

her but that one time, that one time only." He looked away, was silent for a moment in a silence kept by everyone else in the big room. He gazed around at the room, the stretches of brick wall painted different colors, the torture instruments, the body in the barber chair, the glass-jeweled chest of costumes, the mummy case in a far corner. It was as if he were inventorying his life. He turned back to Dave. "Why not Fullbright, then?"

"I guess I'd better go ask him," Dave said.

19

The management didn't waste a lot of money lighting up the Sea Spray Motel at night. It was a bleak pair of oblong stucco boxes facing each other across a blacktop parking lot. The wooden stairs swayed as Dave climbed them. At the top, he squinted up at the white plastic circles set in the roof overhang. He gauged the power of the bulbs they hid to be twenty watts. The gallery he walked along sagged. The merry blue paint on the wooden railings was peeling. The varnish was scaling off the door of unit Twelve. Curtains were across the aluminum-framed window, blue-and-white weave with an anchor. Light was not leaking around the outside of the curtains. But Delgado's wreck of a car was parked below. Dave knocked. Someplace a small dog barked. No one stirred beyond the door. Dave knocked again louder. A door opened across the way. Television sounds came out. The door closed. Dave knocked again. And was rewarded by moans. He felt footsteps thud. The door jerked open.

"What the hell?" Delgado blinked. "Oh, shit. Dave?"

"I'm sorry." Dave looked at his watch. It was nine. "Were you asleep?"

"Yeah, well—informally." Delgado tried for a laugh. "I, uh, dozed off with the television on." He'd lost the crisp, clean look he'd had this morning. There was an orange stain on the front of the white shirt. Pizza sauce? The jeans Dave had lent him day before yesterday were crumpled. "Something on your mind? Something I can do?"

"You thought I didn't mean it," Dave said. Delgado stank of whiskey. The air that came out of the shut-up unit stank of whiskey. "You thought I'd paid your rent and thrown you away. What made you think that?"

"You said the case was over," Delgado said. "You've got your house to fix up. You've got Amanda. You don't have to work—only when you want. How did I know you'd ever have another case? I haven't got forever."

"It will seem like forever," Dave said, "on skid row, sleeping under newspapers in doorways."

"Yeah, well, I can take the stuff or leave it alone. What happened? The son didn't do it after all?"

"I don't know what he did. I need that girl to tell me. And I still can't find her. Odum doesn't know where she is. I'm going to see a man I think maybe does. The last time I saw him, he fell over my foot and broke his nose. I'm about to act very nasty to him. It came to me it might be a good idea to have someone along. Strange as it seems, I thought of you. Are you sober?"

Delgado half turned to peer back into the unit. For a clock? "I don't remember anything after the four-thirty news. That makes four hours. I must be sober, yeah." He looked down at himself. He brushed with a hand at the stain. "I need a shower and a change." His brown dog eyes begged Dave. "Can you wait?"

"You going to let me in?" Dave said.

"It's a mess," Delgado warned him, "a pigpen." But he turned resignedly and Dave followed him inside. The bed was unmade. Soiled T-shirts, shorts, socks, were strewn around. The peeled-back lids of sardine tins glinted in the weak lamplight, the ragged lids of half-empty bean cans, soup cans, crowding a coffee table with merry blue legs and a glass top. A big pizza with one slice out of it drooped in its tin on the television set. A whiskey bottle rolled from under Dave's foot. Its label said it was a cheap supermarket house brand. It clinked against another bottle in the shadows. Delgado said, "I'll make it as fast as I can so you don't have to sit around looking at it." He rattled blue paper laundry bundles on a merry blue chest of drawers and went away into the bathroom.

In a cupboard in the kitchenette, Dave found a dusty box of trash bags. He flapped open one of the big green plastic things and went around the place with it, picking up greasy hamburger, hot-dog, french-fry wrappers, fried chicken boxes, pizza tins, half-eaten candy bars, half-eaten slices of dried-out bread. There were two ashtrays. Both of them overflowed. He emptied them into the bag and with the edge of his hand scraped into the bag the butts and ashes strewn around them. More junk littered the kitchen, beside the sink, under the sink. He stuffed this into the bag too, twisted the neck of the bag, and looped it with the yellow plastic collar the bag-maker furnished. He set the bag on the gallery outside the door.

Food-crusty plates, cups of abandoned coffee, smeared glasses were heaped in the sink. He poked around till he found a bent box of elderly soap powder. Maybe he would startle Delgado in the shower when he ran hot water into the sink, but he took the chance. He didn't hear a yelp, so maybe Delgado was out of the shower by now. Or maybe the management of Sea Spray was more generous with hot water than with wattage. He had to explore again to find a rinse rack. A spider was living in it. He opened the window over the sink and let the spider go down outside on a strand of web. He splashed dust off the rinse rack, set it on the counter, and began drowning glasses in suds and steam. Delgado let out a long low whistle of surprise. He came fast into the kitchenette.

"Hey!" he said. "You didn't have to clean up for me. You don't have to wash my dishes. What is this?"

"You cooked my breakfast," Dave said. "Several times." He shook dust out of a blue dish towel and held it out. "You can dry, if it will make you feel better."

"I never played cleaning woman for you," Delgado said.

"I didn't need it." Dave began setting glasses in the rack. Delgado reached for a glass. Dave stopped him. "You don't know how to be a cleaning woman. Those have to be rinsed, first. Marie spoiled you. And your mother before her, I expect. Just wait a minute."

"Who is this guy we're going to see?"

Dave found a saucepan, ran hot water into it, poured the water over the glasses. "Now you can wipe," he said. He put the pan down and went back to washing dishes. "His name is Fullbright. He and Dawson were partners."

"Where do I put these?" Delgado said.

"On the shelf where you found them when you moved in," Dave said. Delgado looked helpless. Dave opened a cupboard. "There. That should put them in easy reach."

"You never give up," Delgado said, and set a shiny glass on the empty shelf. "Why did you break his nose?"

Dave told him about Fullbright.

Delgado said, "Maybe he owns a shotgun. You didn't go through every cupboard, every drawer. Dawson threatened to expose him for taking money out of the company, for not reporting his under-the-counter earnings to the IRS. Why didn't he break Dawson's neck to keep him from talking? Why didn't he try to wipe out Spence Odum when he realized Odum had heard the quarrel with Dawson?"

"Because it's been twelve days," Dave said.

"Maybe he doesn't look at the news," Delgado said. "He was

surprised when you told him it was Ludwig who was killed by the shotgun blast."

Dave set cups dripping with suds in the rack. "He'd have known the difference." He filled the pan again and sloshed steaming water over the cups to wash the suds off. "Odum's dark, Ludwig was fair. It would take somebody not sure, somebody who'd never seen them together, or never seen Ludwig at all, to mix them up."

"Did you ever think maybe Charleen had the shotgun?" Delgado touched a cup and drew his hand back sharply and shook it. "She'd only seen Odum once."

Dave loaded saucers and plates into the sink. "She couldn't break a man's neck."

"Fullbright could." Delgado picked up a cup using the towel to shield his fingers from the heat, dried the cup, hung it on a hook in the cupboard. "It wasn't just that Dawson was going to the IRS and the police or DA or whatever. You're forgetting—he had Charleen to start with, then Dawson had her."

"I'm not forgetting anything," Dave said. "I'm remembering too much. That's what's wrong."

"Aren't you supposed to do the silverware before the plates?" Delgado asked. "I seem to remember Marie saying—"

"Marie was right," Dave said, picked up handfuls of stainless-steel knives, forks, spoons, and dumped them into the soapy water. "He didn't have anything to do with horses. I don't think he took those records out of his office to keep me from running to the Feds about him. He had to have a likely reason. That was farfetched." There was a bin at the end of the dish rack for silver. He began putting it clean into this bin. The rattling punctuated what he said. "What he was afraid of was that I'd figure Dawson had learned he was cheating him and dealing in smut and had reacted as Dawson would naturally react and I'd figure this was a motive for Fullbright to kill Dawson." He splashed hot water over the shiny knives, forks, spoons. "Which doesn't mean he did kill him."

"Or that he didn't," Delgado said, finishing with the cups. "It

148

could have been everything—fear of Dawson and hatred of Dawson for taking his girl—disgust with Dawson's holier-than-thou pose. I mean—things do add up." Delgado began to dry the stainless steel. "You can take this, you can take that." He opened a drawer and dropped the clean flatware into it. "But then comes the next thing. It's the total that gets you."

"Except—when it gets you, what do you do?" Dave set saucers in the rack, then swabbed off the plates and racked them to drain. He glanced at Delgado. "You give up and drink. Bucky loses control. What would Fullbright do?" He poured steaming tap water over the plates. He felt around in the greasy water that showed a lot of tomato sauce at its edges, found the rubber cover of the drain with his fingers, and pulled it away. He rinsed it off and laid it on the counter. The water went out of the sink with a sucking sound. He rinsed the sink. He took the towel away from Delgado and dried his hands on it. "I know better than to bet on human behavior, but I'm going to do it anyway." He hung up the towel. "Fullbright is in this up to his eyebrows, but he didn't murder anybody."

"You're on," Delgado said. He looked at the plates steaming in the rack. "Are we through here?"

"They'll drain dry," Dave said. "Come on."

20

Most of the boats rocking at the long white mooring were dark, asleep. Here and there, a light showed at a porthole and wavered in the black water beneath. But the lap of tide against hulls and pilings and the hollow knock of their heels on the planks were the only sounds there were until they neared the end of the pier. This was why Fullbright had no near live-aboard neighbors. The loud music from his big white power launch. Not the easy-listening kind that had whispered from the speakers when Dave was here last. This was some kind of rock. No lights showed. Shadowy figures sat around the sheltered afterdeck. The shifting colors of a television screen painted their half nakedness. Teenagers. They sat on the padded bench along the taffrail and giggled and murmured and passed from hand to hand a handmade cigarette. When Dave and Delgado stepped aboard, a blond boy stood up and came to them.

"No admittance," he said. "Private party." He had the bleached eyebrows, the deep tan, the muscles, that made him a lifeguard, a permanent surfer, a beach bum, or all three. The smell of sun came off him. He was taller and broader than Dave and had a wine bottle in his hand. Baggy surfer trunks hung low off his hips and he wasn't steady on his feet. "Please leave," he said.

"This is urgent," Dave said. "Tell Jack Fullbright it's Dave Brandstetter. He'll want to talk to me."

"It's past business hours," the boy said.

"I didn't ask for the time," Dave said. "Go tell Jack Fullbright I'm here, please."

The boy half turned and set the wine bottle down on a low round table among other wine bottles, bowls of chips, bowls of ravaged sour-cream and cheese dips. "I can break your arms," the boy said.

"If you want cop-show dialogue," Dave said, "my friend here is wearing a gun, and if you try to get cute, he will shoot you in the kneecap."

The boy blinked white eyelashes at Delgado. Delgado glowered and put a hand inside his jacket over the rib cage. He told the blond boy, "He means it."

A girl wearing a white Levi's jacket over a bikini came around the table and took hold of the boy's arm. "Ricky, come on and sit down."

"Call him on the gun," a male voice said out of the dark. Another one said, "Yeah, let's see the gun."

Delgado took out the gun, held it up, put it back.

The boy said to Dave, "He told us not to let anybody down there. We can't go down there ourselves. If we have to pee, we pee over the side, right? He's got people down there. He's very busy and doesn't want to be disturbed."

Dave went to the companionway, laid back the hatch doors, pulled open the short, shiny, vertical doors. Light from the brass lanterns down in the cabin made a yellow sheen on the teakwood steps and sent streaks up the brass handrails.

"I really wish you wouldn't," the boy said. "He'll have my ass for this."

"He's probably had that already," Delgado told him.

"That's a sexist remark," Dave said. The children were picking up gear and starting to leave. "Don't go anywhere. He's your friend. He gives you booze and grass. Don't walk out on him when he needs you."

A girl and a boy went anyway. The others stood as they were, doubtful, looking at Dave and Delgado, then at each other. The boy named Ricky said, "Okay. What's it about? Who are you?"

"Private investigators," Dave said. "Working for the insurance company that Jack Fullbright's partner had a life policy with. He was murdered. It's serious, right? So you will wait, won't you?"

They murmured, took steps this way and that way, then one by one sat down. Dave went down the companionway. At the foot of it he stopped. Delgado bumped against him. "Sexist or not," he said, "I was right." He pointed.

The door in the bulkhead separating the cabin with the leather couches and bar and music system, from the cabin with the beds was open, and it showed Dave naked legs waving happily. Slim, shaved legs tangled with muscled, hairy legs. The music was very loud down here. Dave went and turned it off. In the sleeping cabin, a boy like Ricky, long blond hair in his eyes, tumbled onto the floor between the beds. He lay on his back, laughing. He was naked, and a naked girl fell on him. It was Ribbons. They started wrestling, or it might not have been wrestling. Then Jack Fullbright's voice said sharply:

"Wait a minute. Shut up, will you? Something's wrong."

He stepped over the suddenly stilled bodies on the floor and was framed in the doorway. He wasn't wearing anything, of course, except the little silver chain around his neck and a wide slice of adhesive tape holding thick folds of gauze over his nose. The tape went far out across his cheekbones. The flesh around his eyes that wasn't covered by the bandage was black and blue and swollen. He could only open his eyes as slits. They glittered.

"What the hell is this? What do you want?"

He reached around the door for a white terrycloth robe. Ribbons stared amazed at Dave and Delgado between Fulbright's legs. So did the blond boy. He'd tilted his head far back. That it was upside-down made his alarm look comical. Fullbright stepped out of the sleeping cabin and shut the door. He flapped into the robe. It was floor-length and had a hood. He didn't put up the hood. Dave studied his motions. They were slow. He had to be full of painkillers. There was no way, without them, that Fullbright could have amused himself as he'd just been doing only a day after smashing his face on those steps. The pills would have hampered his capacities, but Dave suspected it had taken time and diplomacy and luck to set up this date. Fullbright wouldn't have canceled for anything less than a coma.

"Still the same thing," Dave said. "To know where Charleen is. You lied before. You knew her. You asked Spence Odum to put her in a film. It would cost you but you didn't seem to care. She meant something to you. So where is she, Fullbright?"

Beyond the door behind the man in the long white robe there was a rattling noise. Somebody stumbled on stairs. Dave looked a Delgado and Delgado pushed Fullbright aside, yanked open the door to the sleeping cabin, lunged through. Dave saw the boy's naked legs disappear at the top of a companionway at the far end of the cabin. Delgado had hold of Ribbons. She had on jeans now but no top as yet. She squirmed in Delgado's grip and let out little gasps with words muffled inside them of fear and outrage. She tried to hit Delgado with little thin blue-veined fists. Beyond the far companionway, there was a splash. The boy must have gone overboard forward.

"I'd like the truth this time," Dave said.

Fullbright didn't answer. He watched Delgado bring the struggling, whimpering Ribbons into the after cabin. Delgado set her down hard on the couch. She crossed her arms in front of her little breasts and glared up at Delgado through her tumbled hair. Her mouth pouted.

"I guess you're going to get it, aren't you?" Fullbright dropped disgustedly onto the couch opposite Ribbons. "Or you'll have the vice squad down on me."

"You're a poor judge of character," Dave said. He reached into a pocket and brought out the sheaf of invoices he'd gone off with the last time he left this boat. He flipped them at Fullbright. "I'm going to get it by offering you these back."

"Or you'll take them to the IRS." Fullbright nodded.

"And the police, and the district attorney, and any other agency I can think of that frowns on theft and cheating and embezzlement —to say nothing of murder."

Fullbright shut his eyes, shook his head, grunted, slouched down on the couch, hunching up his shoulders. "I didn't kill him. I felt like it, but I didn't. I figured out another way." A wise smile twisted his mouth at one corner.

"I'm cold," Ribbons said.

"To shut him up and back him off," Dave said, "after he discovered you were renting equipment to porno filmmakers and not even giving him a share of the take."

"It wasn't the money," Fullbright mumbled. "It was the sinfulness of it all. He was going to destroy me."

Dave stepped to him and shook his shoulder. "Don't go to sleep on me. Explain this." He held in front of Fullbright's face the fuzzy photo of wanton Charleen on the motel-room bed. The slits in the bruised swellings opened for a moment and closed again. "You took it, didn't you? Don't tell me why; let me guess. Dawson was with her."

Fullbright nodded slowly. His voice was almost inaudible now. "You know already. Why ask me?" He raised a very slow hand and very gingerly touched the bandage across his nose. "Leave me alone, all right?"

"I'm cold," Ribbons whined, and Delgado went into the sleeping cabin and brought back a white Irish hand-knitted sweater. She put it on. It must have belonged to the boy or to Fullbright. It was

154

much too big for her. She huddled down in it, glowering, sulking.

"You're welcome," Delgado said.

"I found him looking at magazines in his office one night when he thought I'd gone home, only I remembered something I needed and I came back." Fullbright blew out air wearily. "They had pictures of naked little girls in them." A sound came from Fullbright that was almost a laugh. "He put them away fast and I made believe I hadn't noticed. It really shocked me." He looked at Dave for a second and shut his eyes again. "I actually believed the son of a bitch was what he claimed to be. Until then."

"And he thought you still believed it," Dave said, "when he went over to Spence Odum's studio and tore it apart and snatched back all the stuff that belonged to Superstar Rentals. And threatened to wipe you out."

Fullbright nodded even more slowly this time.

Dave looked at Ribbons. "Take Mr. Delgado to the galley and come back with some coffee, please. On the double, as we say on shipboard."

Ribbons gave no sign of doing what he asked. Delgado pulled her to her feet. He pushed her ahead of him through the sleeping cabin.

Dave didn't watch where they went. He asked Fullbright: "You already had Charleen for a little playmate by that time, right? Where did you find her?"

"You wrecked my face," Fullbright said. "It hurt like hell. I'm full of dope. I can't go on with this. I can't figure out what the hell to say."

"Try the truth," Dave said.

Fullbright drew a deep breath and pushed himself a little more erect on the couch. He said loudly, "I found her in a place on Sunset called the Strip Joint, where kids dance and drink soda pop and hustle sex for bucks, for pot, for cocaine, for auditions, for whatever you promise them."

"And you rent stuff to filmmakers," Dave said. "So you have

connections with producers. She thought you could get her into the movies."

"Also I had a boat," Fullbright said. "She hadn't been on a boat before. She thought it was glamorous, only if I took it out she got seasick and if I didn't she got bored." His voice ran down. He blew out breath again and shook his head again. He was having trouble holding it up. "She was about to quit me. Then Jerry found my private records and ripped up Odum's studio and all that." Fullbright shut his eyes and shuddered, hunching down inside the big robe. He fumbled for the hood and pulled it crookedly over his rumpled hair. "Man, I have to sleep. I can't go on with this."

"They're bringing coffee," Dave said. "So you got Odum to promise to put her in a picture by offering him everything he needed free. And in return for that, you got Charleen to lead Dawson into temptation—remembering all those skinny girl children in the sex magazines that Dawson found so attractive, right? And you stationed yourself outside the motel room window and snapped photographs of Dawson he wouldn't like featured in his church bulletin." Dave bent to touch a drawer under the couch. "Using one of the cameras you keep here."

"Most people," Fullbright said drowsily, "don't realize they can have their picture taken in the dark." He smiled wanly to himself. "It shut him up. It backed him off." He whispered a laugh, opened his eyes to the extent that he could open them, and looked at Dave. "It also hooked him on Charleen. He couldn't get enough of her —even though he knew she'd agreed to frame him for me. Nothing mattered but sex with Charleen. He'd gone around all his life lusting in his heart after grammar-school girls—what's the word? —nymphets, right?"

"And keeping hands off," Dave said.

"Yeah, well—" Fullbright's eyes closed again and his chin rested on his chest. "He'd have broken sometime. He sure as hell broke completely when he broke."

Delgado came in with a big Japanese pottery mug of coffee. The

156

hand that didn't hold the mug held Ribbons. Dave took the mug. Ribbons and Delgado sat on the couch again. Rick stood in the companionway. He didn't speak. He only looked. He appeared worried.

"Drink some of this," Dave told Fullbright. He seemed always to have to be doctoring the man. He put the mug at Fullbright's mouth. Fullbright jerked up his head. "I don't want it. There's nothing more to tell."

"Where did Charleen go after Dawson was killed?"

"I never saw her again." Fullbright, as if his hand weighed almost more than he could lift, tried to push the mug away. "I swear it. Think what you want, do what you want. I never saw her again."

"You were going to take those records out to sea and drown them. Is that what you did with Charleen? She was a witness to Dawson's murder, wasn't she? And you couldn't depend on her to keep quiet. You had to get rid of her."

"No. I didn't kill him." Fullbright rubbed his forehead. "What night was it?"

Dave named the date. "Between ten and midnight."

"I was here. I picked up a film from Cascade after I left work and brought it straight here. You can check their records." Fullbright numbly took the mug. He blew at the steam. He sucked up a little coffee and flinched. "Hot. It was *Deep Throat.*" He pointed overhead. A rolled-up movie screen was hooked to the ceiling inside its brown metal tube. "The projector sits over there." He looked at the companionway and saw Ricky. "What is it?"

"I was here that night," Ricky said. "Jude and Pepe were here." He turned and called up the companionway. "Hey! *Deep Throat.* You remember when Jack showed it?"

Jude was the girl in the Levi's jacket and not much else. Pepe was a brown boy a little bit overweight. He was chewing. A smear of white was at the corner of his mouth. Jude numbered the night when Gerald R. Dawson was killed. "It was a Monday," she said.

"I remember because that's my tennis night with my yuck little brother. Believe it, I canceled when I heard what was going down."

"Yeah." Pepe rubbed his crotch and grinned. "Going down. *Es verdad!*"

Jude looked at Dave with her eyes very wide open. "How does she *do* that?"

Ribbons, huddled down inside the big sweater on the couch, kept her sulky look. "Did you ever hear of special effects?" Then she giggled. "Trick photography?"

The children in the companionway laughed.

21

A car he didn't know was parked in the dark by the piled cement bags, the sand heap, the stacked lumber in front of the French doors. He went into the courtyard. The fencing room was lighted up. A stranger was in there. He sat on the bed, phone on the floor at his feet, receiver at his ear. The light in the room was overhead, two hundred watts, a naked bulb, bleak. Dave stood under the white flowers and trailing tendrils of the vine at the back of the courtyard and watched the man through the open door. He was half turned away but he looked young and spare. He wore a brown double-knit suit and shoes that gleamed. His brown hair was cut 1930s style, neat, the latest. He spoke into the phone and Dave thought he knew the voice. He went through the doorway and walked to the bed.

Randy Van looked up and smiled. He picked up the phone, rose, handed Dave the phone, handed Dave the receiver. Dave took them dumbly, staring. There wasn't a trace of makeup. There was no enamel on the nails. Dave said "Brandstetter" into the phone.

"The soil samples from the closet floor at unit number thirty-six," Salazar said, "match the stuff from the clothes of the deceased, Gerald R. Dawson."

"Dandy," Dave said. "Anything else?"

"A lot of fingerprints. Who knows how long it will take to sort them out and get a line on them? Your witness, Cowan, told me she brought pickups there. She must have been busy. She sure as hell was too busy ever to clean the place. But he wasn't murdered there, anyway, Brandstetter. When the neck is broken—"

"The muscles that control bladder and bowels let go," Dave said. "I know that. I also know it doesn't always happen. Only almost always."

"Almost is good enough for me," Salazar said. "I don't want this case and I don't get this case."

"Don't hang up," Dave said, and put a hand over the mouthpiece. Randy was sorting through a stack of record albums on the floor. Dave asked him, "How long have you been here? Any other calls?"

"About an hour. Yes. A Lieutenant Barker of the LAPD. He got the report from the lab where we left that envelope of Karen's. They phoned him, like you asked."

"Did he tell you what they said?"

Randy nodded, studying a glossy color caricature of Mozart with a croquet mallet. "It's decomposed granite. It doesn't match. The other was alluvial." He looked up at Dave. "He's going to the district attorney about it."

"Thanks," Dave said. "You look very nice."

"I feel ridiculous in these clothes," Randy said. "Does that mean the one with the horses gets out of jail?"

"That's what it means," Dave said. "Why don't we drink to that? The cookhouse is over yonder."

Randy got to his feet, and put a kiss on Dave's mouth. "You're a nice man," he said, and went away. He didn't sway his hips.

Salazar whistled into the phone. Dave took his hand off the

mouthpiece. "Sorry," he said, and told Salazar about getting the soil sample from Tooker's place in Topanga and about what the lab had said and about Barker's reaction. "Now—I can ask him to do it or I can ask you to do it, but somebody has to do it," he said.

"What's that?" Salazar said.

"Test Bucky's shoes," Dave said.

"To see if what's on them matches what was in the closet?" Salazar asked. "You know, I don't see how just eating lunch with a guy could do this to somebody, but I'm starting to think like you. And it hasn't helped. I checked out the kid's shoes. Negative. I even showed the kid to Cowan. Cowan isn't so sure now. He says Bucky looks smaller. But maybe it was the light. It was dark before."

"It's still dark," Dave said. "I don't know. I just damn it don't know." He sat on the bed, scowling to himself, chewing his lower lip. Salazar asked him if he was still there. "I don't know where I am," Dave said. "Look, thanks very much. I'm sorry to have put you to all the trouble. I appreciate your cooperation, your help."

"Any time," Salazar said.

"Somebody killed that man," Dave said.

"Not the widow and orphan," Salazar said. "Write them their check and forget it."

"Sure," Dave said, but he wasn't listening. He was thinking about Bucky's size. He asked Salazar, "Are you going to be there for a while?"

"I'm already into my fifth hour of overtime," Salazar said. "I'm going home to bed."

"What about your stolen-property office? Can you leave word with them that I—"

"Nine to five, Brandstetter," Salazar said. "Somebody in this crazy place keeps normal hours."

"I'll see you in the morning," Dave said and hung up.

Randy came back carrying stubby glasses with what looked to

be scotch over ice cubes. He handed Dave one of the glasses. "Does that mean we've got all night?"

"I have something to do before sunrise," Dave said.

"You mean besides right here?" Randy said.

"After right here," Dave said. "You know, you should get dressed up funny more often."

It wasn't sunrise. It was after. But the old black man in the starchy tan uniform sat upright and wide-eyed in his faded blue Corvair next to the driveway ramp down into the garages under Sylvia Katzman's apartment complex. The street was steep and the worn right front tire of the car was turned hard against the curb. Dave put the Triumph into the lowest gear he could find with the stubby shift knob and climbed the hill. He got lost on twisting, narrow, shelflike streets but he found the place he wanted finally, and parked and got out. It was the place where the chain-link fence was cut at the bottom, the corners folded back. He looked down. There were the kitchen windows of the top row of apartments. The one on number thirty-six was still open the way he'd left it on his first visit. It was plain from here that climbing had taken place up the bank. The slant of the early sunlight, already promising heat again, showed up the marks of dug-in shoes or boots. And of something heavy having been dragged. He got back into the Triumph and lost his way again getting back down to the parked Corvair. The old man was drinking coffee out of a red plastic cup that was the cover of his Thermos bottle.

"Yes," he said, consideringly. "I saw a truck like that. Those big wheels that set it up high. Four-wheel drive, I expect. It rumbled. A lot of power."

"Machinery in the back?" Dave asked.

"Oh, yes." The old man nodded. He reached across to a glove compartment held shut by an arrangement of thick rubber bands. He worked these with arthritic fingers. "I have some cups in here."

The metal door of the glove compartment fell open. "Perhaps you'll share a little coffee? Tastes good first thing in the morning." He pulled a cup out of a nest of six and carefully filled it from the Thermos. His motions were slow and tidy. He handed the cup through the window to Dave. "It was posthole-drilling equipment." The old man recapped the Thermos. He put the cups back into the glove compartment and fixed it shut again with the rubber bands. "And on the front, there was an arrangement to attach something, probably a grader for laying down roads, you know?"

"The coffee's good," Dave said. "Thank you. When did you see the truck?"

"It was parked back up there." The old man raised a slow hand to point with a thumb over his shoulder. "I drive up there to turn around and come back down here to park in this space. This is a good old machine but it doesn't have much left in reverse. Two weeks ago?" He wrinkled an already deeply wrinkled forehead. "Not quite."

"It was here when you arrived?" Dave said. "That would be what—seven o'clock in the evening?"

"Right about then," the old man said. He drank coffee and stared thoughtfully through the windshield. He shook his head. "No, that wasn't the first time. First time was Sunday, the day before. Early. I was fixing to leave. Boy with a black beard got out of it. He couldn't get in the building. They have to know you are coming so they can come unlock the lobby door for you."

"Who came?" Dave asked. "Who let him in?"

"Maybe he never got in," the old man said. "He was still standing there when I left. He had on a cowboy hat." Now he looked hard at Dave. "Do you know," he asked, "the Monday when I saw the truck up there—that was the one they been asking me about. The police. The sheriff. Who came and went that night? Yes, sir! They been asking me about that night." A little weary smile twitched his mouth. "But they never asked me one time about that truck. You the first one, the only one."

"But the boy with the beard wasn't in it when you saw it?" Dave asked.

"Nobody was in it. But later on there was. Must've been getting on for midnight by then. He come out and tramped up right here past me, so close I could have stretched out my hand and touched him. He unlocked the truck and climbed in and slammed the door and drove it right on up the street to the top, like you did just now."

"Alone," Dave said. "No skinny little blond teenage girl with him?"

"Alone," the old man said. He sipped coffee and thought again for a minute. "You want to know why I remember that? Why I paid special attention? Him getting in that truck and driving off?"

"Why was that?" Dave said.

"Because he didn't look the same without the beard."

"I'd bet on possibly a wallet," Dave said. "Almost certainly a duffel bag, maybe even Marine or Army issue. And clothes—work clothes, Levi's, chinos, work shoes, maybe cowboy boots. Underwear, probably dirty since he didn't know his way around."

The dark kid in uniform kept pulling cartons and parcels off steel shelving in the big room full of steel shelving. He and Dave looked into the cartons and parcels. When Dave shook his head, the kid pushed the cartons and parcels back in place. "You know," he said, "once I make detective, I'm going to quit and get into your line."

"I won't tell them you said that," Dave said. "You need time to think it over." He reckoned the child's age at about twenty. He was dark, with a rosy flush under smooth skin. "When you've had time, you'll change your mind." A date scrawled on a carton in felt pen made him stop. "Let's look in this one."

"I won't change my mind." The kid pulled the box off the shelf and held it for Dave. "I've read about you in the magazines. I saw you on the 'Tomorrow' show. What you do is what I want to do."

164

"Be in the magazines, you mean?" Dave said. "Be on television? It was twenty years before that happened to me. You know what it's a sign of?" He poked among soiled, crumpled T-shirts and boxer shorts in the carton. White boot socks stiff with sweat. There were no boots, no shoes. But there was a wallet, stitched with thongs around the edges, and tooled with a cross entwined by lilies. The wallet was empty. Dirt-crusty work pants had been folded to lie flat. He lifted them. "It's a sign your best days are behind you." Crushed khaki canvas. A knapsack. US ARMY. He lifted it out, laid back the flap. The book was there. He removed it. "Like the worn-out comedians on game shows."

"You don't look worn out," the kid said. "Is that what you wanted?"

Dave nodded. The kid put the box back on the shelf. Dave said, "Before you get into the magazines and on TV, most of what's cluttered up your life has been boring."

"You didn't make it sound like that," the kid said.

"The boring part you don't talk about," Dave said. The book was eight by ten, not thick but heavy. The cover was sleek stamped fabricoid, blue and gold, the gold partly rubbed off. ESTACA HIGH SCHOOL 1977. "Naturally," Dave said. "People watching the 'Tomorrow' show are sleepy. They only want to hear the exciting parts. Same for the magazine readers." He leafed over pages heavy with glossy coating. A girl's volleyball team under eucalyptus trees, mountains towering in the background. A football team, massive shoulder pads, gangly wrists. The a capella choir in pleated robes. Rows of little square photographs of faces, smiles, no smiles, impudence, dread, determination, defeat, dental braces, acne, eyeglasses, perfect beauty. FROSH. SOPH. JUNIORS. Charleen Sims looked at him. He checked inside the front cover. *Charleen Sims* in pale blue ballpoint, then *Charleen Tackaberry* in dark blue ballpoint, then *Mrs. Billy Jim Tackaberry, 456 Fourth St., Estaca, CA.* She dotted her i's with circles. Dave handed back the book. "Ever hear of Estaca? Know where it is?"

"It means 'stake' in Spanish." The kid pulled the carton out, dropped the book into it, pushed the carton back on the shelf. "So maybe it has something to do with vineyards, right? Wine country? San Joaquin Valley?"

"They should make you a detective pretty fast," Dave said.

"I might be wrong," the kid said.

22

He wasn't wrong. And that put it a long way off. It was nightfall by the time Dave found it, a wide main street with high curbs, most of the windows black in stores of cement block or gaunt old brick. Here and there a neon sign said HARDWARE in blue or JOHN DEERE in yellow or DRESSES in pink. There were three or four spaced-out streetlights on tall new silvery standards. A lone traffic light swung high in a wind that blew hot and probably would blow hot all night. The signal switched from red to green to amber and back to red again but there was no one to pay it any mind. Estaca, or most of it, was home for supper and television.

A young woman with lumpy hips stuffed into blue jeans and with a scarf tied over her hair came out the glass door of a store with bright windows. She opened the cab of a pickup truck, put into it a brown paper sack whose squared-off shape said it held a sixpack, and climbed in after it. PACKAGE STORE, the sign said, which meant that in Estaca you couldn't sit in a barroom and drink. If you wanted alcohol you bought it here and drank it where you could. The pickup rattled off up the block. Dave put the Triumph where it had been, on the bias, nosing the curb, struggled out of it stiffly, and stretched. It was no car to travel far in.

"Brand new, ain't she?" the man inside the liquor store said. He was fat. The T-shirt stretched over his immense belly was printed with a purple bunch of grapes and circling the grapes the fancily lettered words CALIFORNIA WINES. His hair was shaved halfway up the sides and crewcut on top. "Lots of pep, I guess."

"It's funny in wine-growing country," Dave said, "not to be able to go into a saloon." He eyed the bottles on the shelf back of the fat man. He wasn't going to find Glenlivet here. "What about restaurants? Are they exempt?"

"Wine only," the fat man said. "What kind is it? German? Italian? Japanese? No, it ain't Japanese. Funny, you think back. I was a kid, you couldn't kill enough of them. Now everybody buys their cars. People forget."

"Those that can," Dave said. "No—it's English."

"Guess you didn't forget," the man said. "They was our allies. You get there in the war?" He grinned lecherously with tobacco-stained teeth. "Boy, them blackouts was something. Anything could happen to you in them blackouts. Girls in every doorway, down every little alley. You didn't have to know where you was; wherever you was, all they had to hear was you talk American and they was unbuttoning your fly. You didn't get there, huh?"

There was a round wire rack of bottled cocktails. He took down two that alleged they were martinis. They were dusty. The line hadn't made the fat man any money in Estaca. "Just passing through," Dave said. "On the way to Germany." Beyond shelves of bread, crackers, potato chips, tall glass-doored refrigerators held cans and bottles of beer, waxed-paper cartons of milk, wrapped blocks of cheese. Ice cream and yogurt lurked in a frost-lined box with sliding glass tops. He located a plastic sack of ice cubes. "Now I'll be all set if you've got cups." He set the little bottles on the counter by the cash register and the wire rack of jerky beef and jolly, half-empty little yellow plastic packets of cheese sticks, corn chips, nuts. "Paper cups, plastic?"

"You figuring to have a party?" the fat man asked.

"All by myself," Dave said, and watched the fat man waddle off for a long transparent plastic sleeve of cups. "Do I have to take them all?"

"I guess not." The man untwisted the lashing on the end of the tube and took out half a dozen. "That okay? I want the count to come out." Dave nodded. The man began pushing buttons on a cash register. "Army, was it?"

"Intelligence," Dave said.

"Marines, myself," the fat man said. He named off the total and Dave paid him. The man laid the bills in gray metal trays. He handed Dave coins. "Maybe in thirty years they'll be buying Vietnam cars."

"Many boys around here fight there?" Dave pocketed the change and picked up the sack the man had put the ice and cups and bottles into.

"This isn't college-kid country," the man said.

"You know one by the name of Tackaberry, Billy Jim?"

"He wouldn't come in here," the fat man said. "Church would be where you'd find him." Little fat-pouched eyes of no special color looked Dave up and down. "He ain't done nothing, has he?"

"It's an insurance matter," Dave said. "Which way is Fourth Street?"

"I ain't seen him for a while," the fat man said. "Big black beard. Crazy eyes. Used to work for Lembke, farm machinery."

"Married, was he?" Dave said.

"Hell, I don't know. I just know Tackaberry's his name and what he looks like. You couldn't forget either one, could you? Fourth's the next after the traffic light."

"Thanks," Dave said and pushed out the glass door.

"Have a nice party," the fat man said.

169

The house sat back on a quarter-acre with four fruit trees in front of it. A five-foot-high chain-link fence closed the yard off. The windows of the house were alight. It might have started out clapboard or even stucco. What sided it now were asbestos shingles in a silvery green. A double gate opened to a driveway where a camper was mounted on a pickup-truck bed. There was a smaller gate for beings on foot to go through. He parked on the packed dirt in front of that, poked a hole in the bag of ice cubes, put cubes into one of the plastic glasses, and emptied half the contents of the martini jug over it. He set the glass on the dash and smoked a cigarette. He swallowed the martini, poured the rest of what was in the little jug over the ice, and set the glass on the dash again. He got out of the car, worked the latch on the gate, and went up a path of cement squares set in grass to a little plywood front stoop. He rapped on an aluminum screen door. A light went on over it. The inner door opened. A gnarled little man in his fifties squinted at him, didn't like what he saw, started to shut the door.

"Mr. Sims?" Dave said.

"I'm eating and I don't buy anything at the door."

"I don't sell anything," Dave said. "Your daughter, Charleen. Is she here?"

The man narrowed his eyes. "Who wants to know?"

Dave showed him the card in the wallet. "I'm investigating the death of a man whose life was insured by Sequoia. In Los Angeles. A man called Dawson. Your daughter knew him. I think she might be able to shed some light on what happened to him."

"In trouble," the man said. "In trouble, isn't she?" He unlatched the screen, pushed it for Dave to come in. The furniture was cheap and not new but it was clean. Everything stood on a floor of spotless vinyl tile exactly at right angles to everything else. There was fresh wallpaper printed with little pink rosebuds, but nothing hung on the walls. "How the hell did she get to Los Angeles?"

"I thought you could tell me," Dave said.

"Billy Jim sure as hell wouldn't take her there." Sims went into a kitchen where order books and catalogues with shiny color covers were stacked on the table. Also glittering bottles of cosmetics. There was exactly enough space to put a plate so the man could eat. A plate was there and he sat down to it. "I'm the Avon lady," he said without smiling.

"Why wouldn't he take her there?" Dave said.

Mouth full of mashed potato, Sims said, "Sit down if you want. Because he thinks it's wicked. Any big city. I warned her not to marry him. She wouldn't listen." He gulped down the food, Adam's apple moving in his scrawny throat. He nodded at the other straight wooden chair, and filled his mouth again. He talked with his mouth full. "He was all right before he went to Vietnam but he was crazy afterwards. She had her eye on him since she was twelve. He was older, of course. Guess all the girls thought he was something extra. Big and strong, and still he had a smooth way of talking, brighter than your average farm-town kid." Sims stopped, started to push back his chair. "Say, you hungry? You want to eat?"

But Dave had seen the dried-potato-flake box on the spotless kitchen counter, and the open can of Dinty Moore beef stew on the stove. "No, thanks," he said. "The US pulled out of Vietnam in 1973. What kept him?"

"Army hospital. Mental ward. Three years, that's right. And when he come back with that beard and that crazy look in his eyes, I said to her, 'Forget him. Pick somebody else. He's off his head.' But it had been 'Billy Jim' this and 'Billy Jim' that, all the while he was gone. She wrote to him damn near every day. He wrote to her too. Years, I'm talking about, you understand." Sims took his empty plate to a chipped sink with unplated steel faucets. He opened the door of a very old refrigerator. Notes on three-by-five cards were stuck to the door with transparent tape. They fluttered a little when he shut the door. "Ice cream?" he asked.

"No, thanks," Dave said again. He wanted to get back to the

martini chilling in the car. Martinis, plural. He was liking the sound of Billy Jim less and less. "I hoped she might be here."

"Hasn't set foot here since she married him," Sims said. He sat down and ate ice cream directly out of the carton with a spoon whose silver plating was almost gone. "No, that's not true. Jesus Christ!" He got up suddenly and turned away. He did something with his mouth. A glint of pink and white and gold wire rattled on the counter. "That ice cream hits that bridgework, makes you want to scream," Sims said, sat down again, took up the carton and spoon. "No, they lived here a little while. In her mother's old room and mine. Her mother's dead, you understand."

"I'm sorry," Dave said.

"She could handle Charleen. I never could," Sims said.

"Where did they go? Where do they live now?"

"Up the river valley back of nowhere. Had a baby." Sims licked the spoon. "Don't know why he picked her. He could have had his choice of girls." He sighed, closed the ice-cream carton, rose, and shut the carton up in the refrigerator. The spoon rattled in the sink. "Then again, maybe they saw he was mental, the war unhinged him. She didn't care. She was born without caution." He eyed Dave. "You're in a hurry, aren't you? I talk too much. Course, folks around here kind of like that. Nothing much to do. Passes the time. All right, let's see—they lived here till Billy Jim got some money from some aunt of his who died. He didn't like Lembke because Lembke uses foul language and doesn't go to church, and he didn't like me for the same reason. So he quit his job at the farm-machinery place and he quit this house, and I don't see them and I don't hear from them."

"Not even about the baby?" Dave said.

"Oh, about that, yes," Sims said. "What Billy Jim did was buy a mobile home and truck it up there and set it down in the middle of his ten acres of nowhere. He had it worked out in his head how it's developing up there, and maybe it is. And he put the money in machinery to dig postholes and dig wells and lay out roads and that kind of thing. Enough work to keep body and soul together. And he wanted to be away from people. He was forever over at the church before that money came, but after that he didn't seem to mind turning his back on the church folks like on everybody else. Just him and Charleen, that was how it was going to be."

"And the baby," Dave reminded him.

"No. Baby was killed. Windstorm, rain, all of that. Knocked that mobile home flat. He wasn't there, couldn't get there. Charleen was alone. Baby was dead in her arms when he came back and lifted the junk off her.

"Crazy thing to do," Sims said, "go way out there where there's nobody to help if you need help. Hell, everybody needs help in this life." He went back into the bare, rose-papered room. Dave went after him. Sims said, "When I had my heart attack, hadn't been for the folks next door I'd be dead. Heart attack's why I'm the Avon lady. Easy work. I don't need much income. Keeps me moving and gives me something to occupy my time." He pulled open the wooden front door. "No, she never had any caution. And now she's mixed up in some man dying in Los Angeles. How?"

"How did he die?" Dave said. "A broken neck. Someone attacked him and broke his neck."

Sims shook his head. "Maybe Billy Jim's got a point about the cities," he said.

"What's the address up there?" Dave said.

"It's not an address at all," Sims said. "I'll tell you how to get there."

"Did she write to you about the baby?" Dave said. "Telephone you? What?"

Sims peered past Dave out the screen door. "Billy Jim brought it here to be buried from the church. He's a religious fanatic. I didn't tell you that, did I? Not that wanting to bury your own child with a preacher in charge of things makes you a religious fanatic.

I don't mean that. I just mean I didn't tell you before. He's a religious fanatic. I don't hold with that. I don't hold with going to extremes. Take it easy, you live longer. What kind of car is that?"

"A Triumph," Dave said. "British make."

"About as big as a baby buggy," Sims said. "No, they don't have telephones up that way. Now, I have to tell you how to get there."

23

The mountains shouldered up black against the stars. Estaca seemed a long time ago. First the vineyards had stopped, then the sleeping cattle, the red steel fence posts, the barbwire. Now there was only the wind. There was only the worn strip of blacktop, only the little car hustling along it, whipped by the wind, chasing its pitiful outstretched lights. There was only him. It was big country. It was a big, empty night. He wondered if he'd understood Sims, if Sims had made a mistake. The martinis were putting him to sleep, the drone of the engine, the sameness of the rise and fall of the rock-strewn, parched-grass foothills. He switched on the radio. Gospel music twanged at him. He switched off the radio. He checked his watch and was surprised. It wasn't yet eight. He looked up.

And the headlights showed him a tin mailbox on a steel stake. TACKABERRY. He pressed the brakes but he'd been traveling fast and the Triumph went on by. He fought the unfamiliar shift knob, got the car into reverse, backed up to the mailbox. A little dirt trail cut off toward the mountains. He swung the Triumph into it. It ran

175

flat for a while, then started to climb. Chaparral and tumbles of rock showed themselves in the headlights when the track took twists. Dead windfall branches littered the ground under old live oaks. The road grew steeper. He shifted gears. The headlights shone at the sky. Then they tilted downward sharply. And out there, below, in the massive darkness, a tiny light showed.

He stopped the car, dry brush scraping its sides, switched off the headlights, got out and stood to let his eyes get used to the night. Wind blew his hair into them. He pushed it back. The light came from a window. Maybe he made out the shape of a house. It was so far off it was like a toy left by some lost child. He wished there were a moon. But even without its lights, the car would warn them he was coming. It was noisy. Noisier even than the wind where the wind had only scrub and rock to sound itself on. He got back into the Triumph, switched on the headlights again, and drove. *This is a mistake,* he thought.

Three old oaks sheltered the tin house. A tin porch ran along one side. On the other side, a lean-to roofed by stiff rippled plastic put in shadow a tractor and big sharp-edged shapes he couldn't name. He walked around the house in the wind. A generator hummed inside a corrugated iron pumpshack. There was no truck. That made him feel easier. He stepped up on the porch and banged the door. Just the wind—in the oaks, and making the house creak along its riveted seams. He banged again. Nothing. He tried the knob. The door was locked. The windows showed him blackness. He shouted, "Hello! Anybody here?" The wind took his voice out into the dark and lost it.

He stepped off the porch and walked around to the lighted window. It was set high and the glass was opaque. Under the lean-to he found an empty fuel drum and rolled it through the weeds until it stood under the window. He climbed up on it and tried to push the aluminum-clinched panel along in its aluminum groove. It wouldn't budge. He jumped down off the fuel drum and thought he heard a sound. But the wind was rattling the thick

176

plastic roofing of the lean-to, and he couldn't be sure. He stood very still and strained his ears. There it was again. A cat? The sound was thin and plaintive. A hurt cat? Then the wind let up for a second and he heard the sound right and knew that it was human. It came from inside.

"Oh, help. Please? Help me?"

"Hold on," he called, and jumped up on the porch again. But this time the little blade from his key case was no use. It worked the lock in the brass-plated knob all right, but there was another keyhole in the door and nothing he had would even slide into it. When the wind let him, he kept hearing her crying and begging. He went back to the fuel drum, climbed up on it, rapped the glass. "I can't get in the door," he said. "Open the window."

It slid back. He was looking into a very small bathroom—toilet, shower stall, washbasin, mirror. She stood with her back against the door, staring at him, eyes large with fear. Her head was shaved. She was in dirty jeans and a dirty sweatshirt. He wondered only for a second, scared as she looked, why she didn't run. She was chained by the ankles. The ankles were thin, and the skin on them was rubbed raw. When he started to climb in she began to scream. He made a clumsy job of getting through the opening. He damn near fell on his head. And all the time she stood against the door and screamed. He twisted the cold tap handle of the washbasin, filled his hands with water, and threw it in her face. She stopped screaming.

For a few seconds she held her breath. Then she began to make the sick cat noise, a whimpering, keening sound. He knelt at her feet. What clamped her ankles were handcuffs from a dimestore play-detective kit. The chains attached were for holding dogs. They ran under the little veneered doors of the vanity that held the washbasin. He pulled open the doors. The chains were padlocked to the faucet pipes. He used the blade from the key case to unlock the handcuffs. He stood and pushed aside with his foot the chains and cuffs. He reached past her for the doorknob. She cringed away from him, both hands covering her mouth. He turned the knob but the door wouldn't open.

"He puts an iron pipe across it," she said. "I have to stay in here all the time he's gone."

"Billy Jim?" Dave said. "Where is he?"

"Off with the truck, working someplace. I don't too much care. When he's here all he does is read the Bible at me and pray at me." She sat on the closed toilet fixture and rubbed her ankles, wincing. "All that scares me, he could just forget me and never come back and I'd die in here. Or there could be a brush fire. It's dry and all this wind all the time. I'd shrivel up like bacon."

The wind made it hard to hear her. The sheet metal the place was built out of hummed. Dave said, "What right has he got to preach at you? You didn't break any necks. You didn't shoot anybody."

She looked up quickly. "Who are you?" Dave wet a washcloth in the basin and gently wiped the tears from her dirty face. He knelt and washed the sore ankles. She said, "You come from LA, don't you? You're a policeman."

"Gerald Dawson's insurance man," Dave said. "I've been hunting you for days. I almost thought you were dead."

"I been wishing I was dead," she said. "Him treating me like he does. Locking me up. Won't let me eat but once a day. Shaved off my hair. Threw out my makeup. Won't let me wear nothing nice. Not till I repent, he says." Through her tears she looked angry. "It's him needs to repent. All I done was go with men. I didn't kill nobody." She sniffed, unrolled toilet paper, and blew her nose. "And he keeps praying to God to forgive *me.*"

"Your father warned you against him," Dave said.

She shrugged. "I thought it was just he didn't want me to do something I wanted to do. That's how he was. Always at me not to do things. Turned out"—she made a wry face—"Billy Jim was no different. Men."

"Was that why you ran off to LA?" Dave asked.

She said, "We done fine right at the start, there. Lived in my daddy's house. Billy Jim worked at the farm-machinery place. He screamed in his sleep sometimes, and being around people made him sweat. He was always talking about how he wanted us to get out of Estaca, out in the country, alone by ourself. I thought it was the war and the hospital and he'd get over it, thought it was just talk, but it wasn't." She'd been staring at memories. Now she looked up at Dave. "Have you got a cigarette?"

Dave held out his pack to her. He'd crushed it, climbing through the window. The cigarettes were bent. He lit one for her, one for himself. "Go on," he said.

"Why did you want to find me?"

"Because you saw Billy Jim kill Gerald Dawson, didn't you? You have to tell the sheriff, the county attorney."

"How did you know to look for me here?"

He told her about the high-school annual.

"You're smart," she said, but she gave her head a worried shake. "Only you're not too young, and you don't look as strong as he is." She stood up on the toilet seat and gripped the windowframe. "We better get our ass out of here. He comes back and finds you"—she hiked herself up and started wriggling out into the night and the wind—"he'll kill us both."

"Can you make it?" Dave said. "There's a steel drum under the window."

"I see it." She wasn't just small and slim, she was limber and quick. She got out a lot more gracefully than he'd got in. He felt bulky and stiff climbing out after her and tried not to meet her eyes as he mismanaged elbows and knees. When he was on the ground, the wind whipping his hair, he told her, "Wait here," and went back under the rattling roof of the lean-to. He probed in the dark with his little flashlight and found a crowbar. He went back to her. She stood by the fuel drum, blinking against the wind, hands on her shaven skull. "What are you gonna do?"

"Break in," Dave said. "I want that shotgun."

179

The door was one of those with big diamond-shaped panes of amber pebbled plastic in its upper half. He smashed one of these with the crowbar, reached inside and worked the two locks, and turned the knob. He let her go in ahead of him and turn on a lamp beside a couch covered in hard-finish brown plaid. A chair matched it. So did the curtains. The floor was vinyl tile patterned to look like oak. A wooden television cabinet yawned empty of its works. A Bible lay on a coffee table.

"You look for the shotgun," she said. "I'll eat."

She went into a little kitchen and opened a refrigerator and took out a box of eggs.

"You don't know where it is?" Dave said.

"I don't want to. After I seen what it done to that man in that parking lot, I don't want to know. It was like his head exploded."

Dave slid back plastic veneered doors on a shallow storage closet. "You were bad luck for him. You were bad luck for Gerald Dawson. You were bad luck for yourself. Why did you go?"

"What would I stay here for? How would you like it? Ripped the insides out of the TV. Took the radio with him. Said I had to cleanse my soul of all that worldly trash."

Dave groped around on the overhead shelf.

She said, "He got to see the farmers he hired out to, but I didn't get to see nobody. No phone, so I couldn't talk to my school girl friends, not even to my daddy. Nothing to read except only the Bible."

Dave pawed aside hanging clothes to look in corners.

"He wouldn't let me have my movie magazines. Baby come and she was some kind of company when he'd be off in the truck. But then there blew up this big storm in March and caved this junky place right in on top of me and the baby died. I laid all night in the rain holding her, dead."

Dave crouched and beamed the flashlight over the floor. Shoe leather gleamed dully but there was no gleam of a gunstock or a gunbarrel either. He stood and rolled the slide door closed. She was

180

frying eggs. In badly burned butter. He reached around her to shine the light into kitchen cabinets. Soap powders, bottled floor wax, pots and pans. Cans, cereal boxes, dried-soup packets. Mugs, plates. No gun.

"He never once took me into town. He had to go for groceries. He says it was bad for me. Guess he thought I'd make him let me see a movie. Never a week went by in my life I didn't see a movie. Till Billy Jim. I loved to read about the stars. I was pretty once, if you want to believe it." She ran a forlorn hand over her bald scalp. "I was a pom-pom girl. And a good dancer too."

Dave opened a door. A small bedroom was beyond it. There was another of the slide-door wall closets here. He searched it too, and the drawers under it. She said:

"What done it was, when the baby was dead, and he took her into Estaca to be buried, he wouldn't let me come along." From the corner of his eye he saw her empty a terrible brown mess from the pan onto a plate. "You want some of these scrambled eggs? You hungry?"

"No thanks." The shotgun could lie in sections in a dresser drawer. He tried that idea. She talked with her mouth full:

"I'm starved. Cornflakes and milk is what I get. Once a day. I told you that. He wouldn't keep the shotgun in there, not in the drawers." She stood in the doorway, shoveling in the food. "He'd think I'd find it and shoot him when he was sleeping. He don't believe how scared I am of that shotgun."

Dave kept going through the drawers, fumbling under clothes, slamming this one shut, yanking open the next one. He was sweating. He was doing this wrong. Everything about it he'd done wrong. It was stupid to have come here alone. He'd been lucky Billy Jim wasn't here when he drove up. She was right. He'd kill them both. Delgado had a gun. If he hadn't been bright enough to bring Delgado he should have brought Delgado's gun. He shut the last drawer.

"So I packed a suitcase and took all the money in the drawer and

181

got out on the road and put out my thumb. And in Fresno I caught a Greyhound. He never hid money from me. Why would he? No place for me to spend it, not way out here. But it wasn't much. I didn't care. I thought I'd get on television right away."

Dave stood on the bed and pushed a trapdoor in the ceiling. He set the little flashlight in his teeth and chinned himself. The metal joists creaked with his weight. He turned his head to make the flashlight beam scan. Dust was all there was. He dropped back onto the bed. The wind kept the house humming. It was like being inside a drum. He wished it would let up. He wouldn't hear the truck if it came. He pushed past her. He'd seen another trapdoor in the front room ceiling. She said:

"I didn't know how hard it would be. I didn't know much. But some girl I met says you could meet all kinds of show-business people on the Strip. You know where that is? And I did. And I was going to be in a picture, too—if Billy Jim hadn't come found me. I never thought he'd do that. He hated the city, any city. Scared him to death."

Dave chinned himself from the coffee table this time. But the little light didn't show him anything. He dropped.

"I know most of the story," he told her. "What I want to hear from you is how he killed Gerald Dawson."

"I had this apartment." She laid the plate in the sink and opened the refrigerator again and brought out a milk carton. From it she filled a glass. "Real beautiful."

"I saw it," Dave said. "Charleen, we can't stay here any longer. If that shotgun isn't here, then he's got it with him. And that could be very bad news."

Carrying the glass of milk, she went out the front door and stood on the long tin porch. "If he was coming, I'd see him. A long way. Clear to the top of the ridge." She stepped back inside. "You want the shotgun so you can take him back too—is that right? To keep him off you with his hands. To keep him from doing to you what he done to Jerry?"

"Where did it happen? In the bed?"

"In the kitchen." She went back on the porch. "Took hold of him, twisted his head somehow. You could hear the snap, and he was dead. I tried to run out of there." The wind was too loud for him to hear the next sentence. "Way he was hitting me, I thought he'd kill me too. I kicked him and ran out on the balcony but I was dizzy and my legs wouldn't hold me and he yanked me back inside."

Dave threw the cushions off the sofa. He groped inside for the mechanism that let it open into a bed. He found it and moved it. Sheets, blankets, two pillows. No shotgun. He looked around. "I went to that apartment. The sheriff's men went there. There was no sign of his having been murdered there. There should have been a mess."

"There was," she said. "I didn't know that happened to dead people. Billy Jim made me clean it up. It made me sick to my stomach. I kept having to run to the bathroom and throw up."

Dave went out past her. He stepped down off the porch, crouched, shone the little light under the porch.

She said, "But Billy Jim kept after me. Made me mop it twice and clean up all the signs where I washed the mop out, you know. Then he says, 'Now wax it.' And I laid wax on it while he was wrapping Jerry in a tarp from the truck and pulling and hauling his body out the kitchen window. Then I had to help him get it up the hill to the truck. He cut a hole in the fence so we could get through. To the street up above there." She said, "I don't know why. It's not cold. But I'm cold. I have to get a sweater."

There was nothing under the porch. Dave looked toward the dark ridge between this scoop of night valley and the highway. He went in after her. She wasn't getting a sweater. She was in the bathroom. She'd taken down the pipe that crossed the door and barred it when it hung in the bright brackets Billy Jim had screwed into the frame.

"What are you doing?" Dave said.

"I want to look nice," she said. Water splashed.

"Dear God," Dave said. "Charleen, come on. There's no more time."

"I'm coming," she snapped. "Just wait a minute."

"Why did he kill Dawson?"

"For corrupting me," she said through the door. "He warned him first, Sunday morning at the church. Jerry says get lost. So then the next day he phoned Mrs. Dawson what was going on with Jerry and me and for her to come get her husband. I didn't know that till afterwards, didn't know he was hid in my closet when they come—her, and the preacher, and Bucky boy. He was in there before Jerry and me got there. Must've killed him hearing me and Jerry in bed." Something happened to her diction. She was brushing her teeth and talking with the brush in her mouth. "My heart like to stopped when he jumped out of that closet after Bucky boy left. I didn't know him for a minute. He'd shaved off his beard."

"Yes, why did he do that?" Dave asked.

"To fool that old nigger-man guard," she said.

Dave tried the door. Locked. "Charleen, you're wasting time. We have to get out of here."

"Just one more minute," she said, and water ran hard.

"Why did Billy Jim stop at only two men? What about Fullbright? Wasn't he the one who started this whole thing?"

"Billy Jim never let me get to telling him about Jack. And when I seen what he done to Jerry and Mr. Odum, I wasn't about to tell him. That fancy boat, marijuana, cocaine, him taking them dirty pictures of me—he'd want to kill Jack Fullbright twice. I was so scared that night, I almost—"

She screamed. And it wasn't about memories. It was about now. Glass shattered. A male voice spoke words Dave couldn't make out. There was a heavier crash. He recognized that one. The top of the toilet tank. Billy Jim was dragging her out through the window. Dave ran across the meager living room and out at the door with the broken pane. The big, blocky pickup truck stood twenty steps off, engine rumbling, headlights dark. Of course. Billy Jim had seen the house lit up, seen the Triumph in the yard, known something was wrong. The trail down here wouldn't have been strange to him. He could drive without lights all the way from the ridge.

He appeared under his cowboy hat from around the corner of the wind-rattling house, dragging the kicking, screaming, stick-thin little girl toward the truck. Cowan was right. He was stocky like Bucky but bigger. Heels clattering, Dave ran along the porch. *You're not too young,* she said again inside his mind. And he launched himself at Billy Jim Tackaberry. Not bad for an old man. He got both legs just at the knees. The knees buckled. All three of them rolled in the dust. But Dave couldn't hold on. Tackaberry got a leg free and kicked Dave in the head. Hard. Dave didn't see anything or hear anything. Then he heard a gonging sound. Something had banged the body of the truck. He heard grunts, squeaky cries. His head hurt.

He groaned and moved. He got to his hands and knees and collapsed again. The truck door slammed. The big engine roared. Dave staggered to his feet. The truck came at him. He threw himself out of its way, tumbling among crackling brush. The truck hit the porch. A metal prop gave, the roof sagged with a shriek, the metal flooring buckled. The truck rocked. Its big gears clashed and ground together. The truck shot backward. The wide tires grabbed at the dirt. Dust kicked up and the wind ripped it away. Dave scrambled for the house, stumbling, falling, on his feet again. The truck skidded in a half-circle and chopped to a halt. Dave turned in the doorway. Light from the truck's instrument panel glinted along a shotgun barrel. Dave fell down, arms over his head. The explosion was big and bright. His sleeves shredded. His arms felt as if he'd stuck them into fire.

The truck roared off.

24

He tried to tell his father, "You can't criticize me. I only did the same thing you did." But his father was dead. And he couldn't form the words anyway. He heard the sounds he made. No more than mumbling. His father faded into the dark. Dave heard a squeak of rubber soles. A door clicked open. Light struck his eyelids and he opened his eyes. The light was hard, dazzling, painful. It glared off white walls. A big bottle hung above him with blood in it. A tube drooped down to him from the bottle. The bottle glittered. He shifted focus. A nurse, plump, middle-aged, no makeup, rimless glasses gleaming, looked at him from the foot of a white bed. Then another face came between him and her, a ginger-moustached young man in a tan uniform.

"Brandstetter? Who shot you?"

"Passed out and drove off the road, did I?" The words came out of him very faintly but his diction was back. "Tackaberry, Billy Jim."

"Loss of blood," the officer said. "Tore up your arms. What did you get blood all over your car for? That's a beautiful car, brand new. Why didn't you phone for help?"

Dave raised his arm to look at his watch. The arm was wrapped in white. The watch wasn't on it. "What time is it? Dear Christ, how long have I been here?" He tried to sit up. The nurse made a sound. The officer pushed him back on the pillows. "Where am I?" Dave said.

"Estaca," the officer said. He read his own watch. "How long —two hours, two and a half?"

"Ah, no," Dave said.

"The doctor had to sew up your arteries. That's why you have to lie still," the nurse said strictly. "You lost a great deal of blood."

"I need to phone," Dave said. A telephone crouched on the table next to the bed. His bundled forearms lay on the blanket. Only the fingers stuck out of the bandages. He worked them. That was all right. "Los Angeles. Lieutenant Jaime Salazar. LA County Sheriff's homicide bureau."

"You're in good hands here," the officer said.

"I believe it," Dave said. "But Tackaberry's going to kill somebody down there." He rolled on his side, started to reach for the phone. The nurse put his arm back. There was no pain. "They used locals," he said to her. "Was I that far out? What did I do, hit my head?"

"You should have worn your seat belt," she said.

"I'll phone for you," the young officer said.

"It's in the building on Temple Street," Dave said. "If he's not there, get them to patch you through to his home. Tell him—"

"You can tell him." The officer nodded at the bedside phone. "After I get him. Who's the target?"

"Jack Fullbright. He lives on a boat at the marina."

"Salazar?" the officer said. "I'll try." He went out of the room, and a tall child dressed like a doctor came in. He cocked an eyebrow, turned down the corners of his mouth approvingly. "You look okay for somebody who almost bled to death."

"Good. Then I can go. It's urgent." Dave tried to sit up again and was pushed back again. The doctor put the cold round circle of a stethoscope to Dave's chest. He shifted it. Again. He took the ends out of his ears. He pulled up the lid of Dave's left eye, right eye. Dave said, "It's a matter of life and death."

"You're a private investigator," the tall child said. "That's pretty romantic."

"It's life and death just the same," Dave said. "Two men are already dead because an Army hospital let a soldier out of the rubber room before he was ready. Tonight he tried to kill me. And he's on his way to—"

The door opened and the officer with the ginger moustache came in. "Salazar isn't at his desk. And your name isn't on the list of people they patch through to him at home. So who else?"

Dave told him about Ken Barker. "There's an address book with phone numbers in it in my jacket. Have you got my jacket?"

"What's left of it," the officer said.

"Well, if you can't reach Barker," Dave said, "please call John Delgado. He works with me."

The doctor took the telephone off the table and carried it to the windowsill and left it there. He said to the officer, "You do all the phoning—not him."

"I'm leaving," Dave said, "when that bottle's empty."

The doctor said, "You have a concussion. I'll want you here till Saturday."

"Splendid," Dave said. He looked at the ginger-moustached youth. "Okay. Please tell Barker to get down to the marina and arrest Jack Fullbright. He's got drugs on that boat. He's probably in bed with an underage kid. The idea is to get him into jail where Billy Jim Tackaberry can't get at him."

"Has this Tackaberry got a license number?"

"It was too dark," Dave said, "and I was busy. You can get the number, can't you? And will you hurry and get Barker, please? LAPD. Homicide division."

"Right. We'll get the license number too. He tried to kill you, right? And you'll swear to that, right? So I'll put out an APB."

"Good," Dave said. "Only get Barker first, okay?"

But he couldn't get Barker. Barker had gone on a trip.

"So I tried your man Delgado. Nobody answers."

Dave looked at the bottle. The blood was dripping into him very slowly. The nurse touched the bottle. She touched the place where it was taped to the inside of his arm just above the bandages. Dave said to the officer, "There's another number in there. Amanda Brandstetter."

"That'd be your wife. You want me to tell her what happened to you? You want her to come and get you?"

"What's the matter?" Dave said. "Won't my car run?"

"It's all right," the officer said, "if you don't mind all the blood."

"Don't tell her what happened to me," Dave said. "Just tell her I got tied up here. Ask her to find Johnny Delgado and get him down to the marina. For the purpose I've already outlined, all right? To get Jack Fullbright off that boat and hidden someplace where Tackaberry can't blow him up with that shotgun. Tell her Johnny will be in a bar someplace near the Sea Spray Motel in Santa Monica."

"That doesn't sound like it would work very well," the boy with the ginger moustache said.

"Then you make an official connection to the LAPD," Dave said. "They'll act for you when they wouldn't for a PI—not even a PI who's been shot."

"You don't know Tackaberry's really going there." The boy looked uncomfortable. "I'd have to clear it with the chief. Tackaberry could be running for Mexico."

"Forget it," Dave said. "We wouldn't want to get the chief out of bed."

"If he got LA all upset and nothing happened, it could be embarrassing for me," the boy said.

"There's another number in my book. Randy Van. Tell him I got smashed up. He'll go down and warn Fullbright."

"Has somebody named Randy Van got muscles?"

"Enough to pick up the phone," Dave said.

"I did put out the bulletin," the boy apologized.

"It's all right," Dave said. "Just phone Van now."

The boy went and the doctor looked in. "Nurse? I want him to have something to make him sleep."

She left, rubber soles squeaking. Dave detached the tube from his arm. His watch, wallet, and keys were in the drawer of the table that had held the phone. His clothes weren't in the closet. He pulled back the loosely woven yellow-orange curtains at the window. Estaca looked as lively as when he'd come through earlier. Trees tossed shaggy in the wind, silhouetted against a streetlight. A step sounded in the hall. He went into the bathroom and turned the lock. Knuckles rapped. "Are you all right?"

"Fine," he said. "I'll be out in a minute."

And he was. Out the window. The short, starchy hospital garment tied in the back wasn't what he'd have chosen to travel in but it was all there was, and the citizens of Estaca weren't looking. By now they'd have switched off the TV and gone to bed. He rounded a sharp stucco corner of the one-story hospital, and there was the parking lot. In the moving shadow of a tree, the Triumph waited for him. The blood on the leather bucket seat had dried in the hot wind. It crackled when he sat on it. The carpet under his bare feet was spongy, sticky. Blood had splattered the instrument panel and the windshield. The steering wheel was crusty with it. He drove into the street. The swinging traffic light showed red but he ignored it.

The big waterside restaurants loomed up dark out of their spotlit landscaping, wide windows glossy black mirrors. The condominiums stood up tall and black against the stars. His watch said it was almost three. He was dizzy and sick and his arms hurt. It was cold here and damp, and he shivered. He stopped the car at the gate to the parking lot where the live-aboard people left their cars. The candy-striped steel pole across the entry was snapped off. He looked at the little white gate house. He thought no one was in it and then he saw the big foot that stuck out the door. He left the Triumph. The guard's hat was over his face. He was folded awkwardly on the cramped floor. His hand was on the butt of his holstered revolver. A bloody hole was in his chest. Dave stood over him and used the telephone.

Then he ran across the parking lot. He ran out the pier. The tender soles of his feet kept picking up pebbles and making him limp. He kept brushing them off. The boats all slept dark on their tethers, lifting a little and falling a little with the lift and fall of the tide. It was deadly quiet. Light streamed up out of the companionway that opened from the deck of Fullbright's power boat. Dave swung aboard. He went down the companionway. No one was in the room with the couches and the bar. But the door in the bulkhead was open to the sleeping cabin. He saw the blood first and then Fullbright's body naked halfway into the washroom where no light burned. He touched the body. It was almost cold. He turned to get away from the blood smell, the slipperiness of the blood underfoot. And he heard splashing. He went up the companionway.

Below, over the side, someone feebly coughed. Someone retched seawater. Someone tried to call out. It came to Dave as a moan. He peered down into the water. Light fell from the portholes of the forward cabin but it only wavered in the water and showed him nothing. The weak splashing came from farther astern. He went back there. The light that reached out here from the parking lot was just bright enough to make the black water hard to see. He blinkered his eyes with his hands.

"Where are you?" he shouted.

"Help!" A white thing floated below. A rope lay on the polished planks. He lowered it. "Help!"

"Can you grab that?" He wound it around an upright and knotted it. "The rope. Grab it." But nothing was happening. Even the feeble splashing had stopped. He heard bubbles break. He went over the rail. The water was cold. The white thing drifted near him, sinking. He groped out for it. Cold human flesh. He grappled for a hold, found limp arms, a hard round skull. He needed to breathe and he let go and surfaced and heard far-off sirens. He smiled, filled his lungs, and went under again.

This time he got hold of the white figure and kicked and the two of them shot to the surface. His arms were around the ribcage from the back and there was no sign of breathing. Clumsily, one-armed, he pushed at the water, bumping the slippery curved hull of the boat, trying to reach the pier. The water deafened him. He heard the sirens. The water deafened him again. The water had soaked through the bandages. The pain from the salt was bright and fierce. He struck a piling with his head. He grabbed the piling and clung onto it.

He took a deep breath and shouted.

And he felt the pier shake with running feet.

It was Randy Van in a soaked white eyelet dress with a long smear of tar on it. He lay on the white pier planks and looked pale green and dead. Except for his legs. The flesh of his legs was lacerated and oozed blood. Paramedics worked over him in green coveralls, nightmare figures in the light from the open hatch of Fullbright's boat. One of the paramedics, a plump black with rolls of fat at the back of his neck, had his mouth over Randy's mouth. A white one in shell-rim glasses sat astride his hips, pressing hands to his lower chest. Somebody wrapped Dave in a blanket and asked him what was funny. Dave couldn't tell him how Randy would enjoy the situation if he knew about it. Dave's jaws seemed to be locked. It was cold. He was shivering so hard it felt as if his joints would come apart. He wished they had more blankets.

Randy made a sound. Water came out of his mouth. His eyelids fluttered. The torn legs kicked weakly. The black and the boy in glasses put him on a chrome-plated gurney and ran pushing it up the pier past staring people in bathrobes toward the parking lot where lights winked amber on and off atop police cars, and a light spun round and round atop an ambulance. The one in the green coverall who had put the blanket around him pushed him down. He was weak and he went down easily. He tried to say that he could walk but the shuddering wouldn't let him. He was pushed flat. His legs were hoisted. Then came another blanket and that was fine. He shut his eyes and the little wheels jarred over the planks. It went on so long it put him to sleep.

Amanda said, "My God, look at his arms! Dave!"

He opened his eyes. She was kneeling beside him. She had on a little pearl-gray derby. He said, "What the hell are you doing here? I only asked you—"

"To find me." Delgado swayed above her, unshaven, eyes bloodshot, shirttail out. His speech was thick. "To get me down here to rescue Fullbright. Only I couldn't find the fucking boat. All I did was get lost. I'm sorry, Dave."

"Not half so sorry as Fullbright," Dave said.

Ken Barker said, "They caught Billy Jim and Charleen in Chatsworth. It was the APB from Estaca that did it." He wore a sheepskin coat, leather side out. "I'm sorry they shunted your call off. I wasn't on any trip."

"I'm glad everybody's sorry," Dave said.

"Why didn't you say you were hurt?" Amanda said.

"I'm all right," Dave said. "It was two hundred miles from here. What could you do?" They were wheeling the gurney. Toward the gaping doors of the ambulance. The legs folded with a mild clacking sound and for a half second he was airborne. "Stop looking so scared," he called back to her.

"We'll follow you," she called.

The ambulance doors slammed shut. It was bright inside. The fat black paramedic hung up bottles of plasma. The siren moaned into life. The engine thrashed. The ambulance began to move. The black found a vein inside Randy's elbow and shoved a big, bright, hollow needle into it. He did the same to Dave. That place in Dave's arm was bruised and Dave passed out for a second. The tubes and bottles swung with the sway of the ambulance. Dave looked across at Randy. He wasn't corpse-green anymore. He smiled wanly at Dave.

"Thank you," he said. "Nice swim."

"I didn't plan for you to get shot up," Dave said.

"It was my own fault. I wasted time changing."

"Why a white eyelet dress?" Dave asked.

"I thought the sensible thing for him to do would be put out to sea. I mean, wasn't that logical? And, well, what else would you suggest a young lady wear for a cruise on a warm summer night?"